Fortune's Heirs

Meet the Fortunes—three new generations of a family with a legacy of wealth, influence and power!

Reed Fortune: The rugged rancher thought being jilted by his fiancée was disastrous enough, but when he woke up married to a beautiful stranger he knew he was in real trouble…

Mallory Prescott: After the blue-blooded debutante had run away from the altar–and a forced marriage–she found herself in the protective care of Reed Fortune…as his mistaken bride. It wasn't long before Mallory realised that she wanted to love her groom forever!

Brody Fortune: His heart had turned to granite after his college sweetheart walked away from him. Would her unexpected return reveal the decade-long secret that had kept them apart?

To Steve and Kenny
–With Love

KAREN ROSE SMITH

spent free time on a relative's farm when she was growing up. She remembers a bull with a ring in its nose, a recalcitrant yearling and the wide expanse of pastures with horses grazing that drew her as a child and still beckons to her now that she is an adult. Pennsylvania is far from Texas, but she called up those memories and they swept her onto the Double Crown for this romance. Karen likes to hear from her readers. You can write to her at PO Box 1545, Hanover, PA 17331, USA.

MARRY IN HASTE...

Karen Rose Smith

Silhouette and Colophon are registered trademarks of Harlequin Books S.A., used under licence.

First published in Great Britain in 2001
Silhouette Books, Eton House, 18-24 Paradise Road,
Richmond, Surrey TW9 1SR

Special thanks and acknowledgement are given to Karen Rose Smith for her contribution to the Fortune's Heirs series.

© Harlequin Books S.A. 1999

ISBN 0 373 65042 6

117-0701

Printed and bound in Spain
by Litografia Rosés S.A., Barcelona

'ARE YOU MY BROTHER?'

Dapper millionaire groom Ryan Fortune received one wedding gift even more awe-inspiring than a diamond-studded champagne bucket –the shocking appearance of his long-lost half brother, Australian mogul Teddy Fortune. Recent Fortune scandal has been tabloid fodder worldwide. Teddy, seeing reports of Texans with his own crown-shaped birthmark, put two and two together and got *millions* …and a whole new clan.

Here's the scoop on Teddy's eyebrow-raising past: over fifty years ago when the now-mythic King Fortune was fighting overseas in World War II, his first wife died of pneumonia, leaving two-year-old son Teddy prey to King's evil father-in-law, who spirited his tiny grandson off to the remote outback. Though King searched mercilessly for his firstborn son, he had vanished without a trace. Until he upstaged the most lavish wedding of the new millennium! Teddy, you really should have called first…

Did we mention Teddy brought some of his children to Red Rock…single sexy heirs with accents! And rampant rumour has it that last night, new-to-the-States rancher Reed Fortune wandered off to a Reno bar to observe the 'local mating customs.' Not only did he wake up in bed with 'the American Dream'–he'd married her! What, pray tell, does an Aussie hunk do for a *second* date?

Fortune's Heirs is a marvellous new set of linked novels that feature the fabulously wealthy Fortune family—their lives, their loves, their dramas and their secrets!

January 2001
Million Dollar Marriage Maggie Shayne

February 2001
The Baby Pursuit Laurie Paige
For Her Baby's Sake Marie Ferrarella

March 2001
A Willing Wife Jackie Merritt
Corporate Daddy Arlene James

April 2001
Snowbound Cinderella Ruth Langan
The Sheikh's Secret Son Kasey Michaels

May 2001
An Innocent Woman Stella Bagwell
Here Comes His Bride Sandra Steffen

Fortune's Heirs

Membership of the glamorous Fortune family has its privileges...and its price! But even the wealthy Fortunes can't buy love—that comes naturally!

KINGSTON FORTUNE (d)

1st marriage
PATIENCE TALBOT (d)

2nd marriage
SELENA HOBBS (d)

TEDDY§ m FIONA BRADLEY — MAX — 13. REED — 14. BRODY — CHRISTOPHER — 15. MATILDA — 16. GRIFFIN

MIRANDA m Lloyd Carter (D)

RYAN

1st marriage
JANINE LOCKHART (d)

KANE — 8. GABRIELLE

2. VANESSA*** — 10. VICTORIA

4. DALLAS
m
Sara Andersen

12. ZANE

3. CRUZ   4. MAGGIE
m
Craig Randall

Travis

†ROSITA AND RUBEN PEREZ

Anita   Carmen   Frieda

MATTHEW
m
Claudia Beaumont

Bryan

2nd marriage
SOPHIA BARNES

CLINT LOCKHART
brother of
6. JACE LOCKHART

CAMERON (d)
m MARY ELLEN LOCKHART

1. HOLDEN 5. LOGAN 7. EDEN

Sawyer*

LILY REDGROVE
m
Chester Cassidy (d)

11. COLE* 9. HANNAH   MARIA

James a.k.a. Taylor

TITLES:
1.	MILLION DOLLAR MARRIAGE	9.	HERE COMES HIS BRIDE
2.	THE BABY PURSUIT	10.	IN THE ARMS OF A HERO
3.	FOR HER BABY'S SAKE	11.	WEDLOCKED?!
4.	A WILLING WIFE	12.	HIRED BRIDE
5.	CORPORATE DADDY	13.	MARRY IN HASTE...
6.	SNOWBOUND CINDERELLA	14.	THE EXPECTANT SECRETARY
7.	THE SHEIKH'S SECRET SON	15.	SHOTGUN VOWS
8.	AN INNOCENT WOMAN	16.	TO LOVE AND PROTECT HER

*   Child of affair
d   Deceased
D   Divorced
m   Married
***   Twins
¦   Affair
†   Loyal ranch staff
§   Kidnapped by maternal grandfather

Prologue

Reed Fortune, his tan Stetson tilted low on his forehead, leaned close to Brazen Spirit's neck as he urged the black stallion into a dead run. The Texas range sped by in a blur. Air rushed at Reed's face as he felt the raw power of Spirit under him. Nothing he did this afternoon helped to ease the betrayal and anger he'd felt since receiving the letter from his fiancée Stephanie back home in Sydney, Australia— not unloading hay into one of the Double Crown's barns, nor working green colts, nor this mad dash across Texas range land.

He and the horse, one in speed and motion, left behind a trail of dust as they raced past mesquite and scattered live oaks. But the early June sun beat down on them relentlessly, and Reed knew he had to think about Spirit if not himself. The fine quarter horse had been a gift from his uncle when Reed had arrived two months ago. Actually Ryan Fortune, patriarch of the family, had told him to take his pick of the horses the Fortunes bred, raised and trained. Reed had taken one look at this restive three-year-old stallion and decided he'd found his mount for at least the duration of his stay.

Reining in Brazen Spirit lightly, Reed slowed him to a lope as he turned toward the fence line leading back to the Double Crown. Then he caught sight of a horse and rider approaching. From the tilt of the rider's hat and his chestnut mount with the black mane, Reed knew it was his cousin Zane. Zane was an executive in the Fortunes' office complex in San Antonio and lived in the city. But often on weekends he and his wife Gwen and their children came to the Double Crown to relax and spend time with the Fortune family.

Reed brought Spirit to a walk to cool him down.

His cousin's usual smile was absent as he rode beside Reed and glanced at him with some concern. "Are you planning on entering Spirit in a race?"

Lifting his Stetson, Reed ran his shirtsleeve across his brow, then resettled his hat on his blond hair. "We were just letting off some steam."

"I hear you've been doing that all afternoon. What's gotten you so riled up?"

Reed figured he might as well tell Zane because everyone would find out soon enough. "Stephanie married another bloke. The news came in the mail today."

Zane pulled his horse up. "You've got to be kidding."

Reed kept Spirit walking.

When Zane brought his horse up beside Reed's again, he asked, "She didn't warn you? No phone call? Nothing?"

"Just a short letter and an apology. No explanation. Dammit, Zane. She didn't even give me a chance to fight for her! If she'd told me something was wrong, I wouldn't have left. If she'd told me something was wrong, I would have gone back. But she didn't give me the chance *or* the right." He swore again, long and hard, his voice as gritty as the Texas dust.

They rode in silence for a stretch until Zane asked, "*Are* you going to go back?"

Reed had planned to stay at the Double Crown until the end of the summer, not only to get to know his long-lost family but to get a good grasp of the horse operation here. Once back home, he'd like to convince his father to expand and modernize their horse-breeding business on the Crown Peak Ranch near Sydney. While he was in the United States, he also wanted to do some traveling. He'd planned to leave tomorrow to go hiking in Big Bend National Park. But now—

Answering Zane's question, he decided, "Stephanie's married. Going back home isn't going to change that." He'd known four or five months was a long time to be separated from her. But they'd discussed it before he'd left and agreed they had the rest of their lives together.

He'd have to tell his family about the breakup. None of his siblings had been very enthusiastic about Stephanie, and he'd thought it was because he'd be the first of the six of them to break away and marry. Stephanie would have made the perfect wife. Living with her parents and helping on their ranch, she had no desire for a career and just wanted to be a wife and mother. Usually quiet, she never argued with him and never did the unexpected. Until now.

As he and Zane walked their horses over the rolling plain and crested a hill, the barns and sheds and training arena of the Double Crown came into view. But before they made the gentle descent, Zane stopped again. "I think you ought to change your plans. Instead of leaving for Big Bend tomorrow, why don't you go someplace a little livelier."

"Such as?" Reed asked, knowing from the look on Zane's face that he probably had something particular in mind.

"A friend I went to college with opened a country-western bar in Reno. It's a great place. Dawson and I went up there a few times in my bachelor days."

Dawson Prescott was a financial analyst for Fortune TX, Ltd., and a good friend of Zane's. "Reno, Nevada?" Reed asked.

His cousin grinned. "Yep. Casinos, shows, women. What more could a single guy want? Why go to Big Bend when you can find a desert like that when you go back to Australia? You can fly the company jet. I'm sure Dad won't mind if you take it up to Reno for a few days or even a week."

Reno. Bright lights, music, women. Maybe Zane was right. Maybe it was time to forget responsibility for a few days and just have some fun. Maybe if he drank enough tequila and danced with enough women he'd forget about a future that had slipped through his fingers.

He'd forget about a fiancée who had chosen someone else.

One

Mallory Prescott pushed open the heavy wooden door, thinking that she'd been a good girl all her life. Where had it had brought her?

To the Golden Spur Saloon in Reno, Nevada.

This should have been the night before her wedding, but thank goodness it wasn't. Running away from what amounted to an arranged marriage to a ruthless man might not have been the most courageous thing she'd ever done, but it was certainly the wisest. Her stepfather had introduced her to and promoted her engagement to Winston Bentley IV, a wealthy San Francisco land developer. From the first moment she'd met him, Winston had been charming, a perfect gentleman and everything Mallory should want in a man. But his kisses had never turned her on and finally, three days ago, she'd questioned her decision to marry him.

Why should she marry a man to earn her parents' approval? And after the phone conversation she'd overheard…

Put it out of your mind, she told herself. *Rebel and have some fun.*

As she stepped into the Golden Spur, she felt as if she'd stepped back in time. There was a wooden bar with an old-fashioned mirror behind it. Lariats, spurs and other Old West memorabilia hung on the wall around it. It was almost nine on a Friday night and the place was packed. The bar stools were full, and couples crowded the dance floor. The woman singing with the country-western band belted out a Reba McEntire tune.

Mallory's half brother had recommended this place if she ever wanted to take a trip to let loose instead of feeling trapped by her engagement. Dawson knew the proprietor and had told her to just mention his name and Matt Conroy would make her feel right at home. Right now she didn't have a home—only her car, a small nest egg and the hope that Dawson would welcome her to San Antonio, Texas, and help her start a new life there. On her way to Reno she'd tried to call him, but she'd gotten his machine. She knew he often took business trips for Fortune TX, Ltd., where he worked. Hopefully she'd reach him in the morning.

But for now....

Her long brown hair, which hung straight to midway down her back, slid across her shoulder as she walked to the bar with her white sundress swirling around her legs. It took only a brief conversation with the bartender to learn Matt Conroy had left early tonight and she was on her own.

On her own. What an exciting thought!

As she looked around the saloon again, she realized that not only was it packed, but every table was filled. She saw one vacant chair at a table where a blond cowboy sat. His jeans-clad legs were long. He was lean, with broad shoulders and a rugged face—a strong jaw and high cheekbones. His skin was tanned, his thick blond hair brushing the collar of his snap-button shirt.

Just as she wondered about the color of his eyes, he raised his head and their gazes met. Blue. His eyes were an unusual light blue rimmed with black, intense in their scrutiny. As her breath caught, her heart gave an unexpected lurch. Suddenly a smile slipped across his lips and he motioned to the chair beside him. Her pulse raced, and she was glad she had taken the time to check in at the motel down the street to change before coming here…because her fun was going to start right now.

When she reached the chair, he stood and held it for her. "Last seat in the house," he said with a grin.

She immediately recognized his distinctive drawl as Australian. "No one is sitting here?" she asked.

"I'm here alone, if that's what you're asking." He extended his hand to her. "The name's Reed."

His hand was large and warm and callused, and she felt terrifically feminine gazing up at him. He had to be at least six-feet-two.

"Mallory," she said softly, deciding she liked the feel of his skin on hers, the appreciation in his eyes, the scent of a musky cologne.

He nodded to the chair he was holding. "Better take it before someone else steals it."

She laughed and sat. He lowered himself into his chair and his knee brushed hers. It wasn't much contact, but it sent a tingle through her whole body. What was wrong with her?

"You looked a little lost. Haven't been here before?" he asked.

"No. I just arrived. How about you?"

"I got to Reno yesterday and spent some time here last night. It wasn't quite as busy. What can I get you to drink?" He motioned to a waitress.

It seemed as if she'd found a gentleman, the way he'd held her chair and introduced himself and now wanted to order for her. Winston had been a gentleman, too. Or so she'd thought. She almost cringed, thinking about how close she'd come to marrying him. She sighed, and to the cowboy's question answered, "I should be having a champagne toast right about now."

Reed cocked his head and studied her. When the waitress stopped at their table, he said, "Bring us your finest bottle of champagne."

"Oh, no," Mallory protested. "Champagne goes straight to my head."

He chuckled. "That might not be such a bad thing."

Those blue eyes were so knowing that her comment about a toast had maybe told him too much. But what could a glass of champagne hurt? Her motel was right down the street, and she could leave here anytime she wanted. "All right, champagne it is."

After the waitress had gone, Mallory could feel Reed's gaze as it drifted from her bangs, over her face, to the thin white straps of her sundress and its embroidered bodice. When Winston had looked at her, she'd felt...like a possession. When this man looked at her, she felt altogether a woman.

But it was a scary as well as an exciting feeling, so she asked him, "You're from Australia?"

"How could you tell?"

His tone was wry and that slip of a smile on his lips once more made her stomach somersault.

A flush crept into her cheeks.

"Sorry," he said with amusement in his tone.

"I'm used to teasing my younger sister. I was born and raised near Sydney. What about you?"

"San Francisco. But I'm on my way to San Antonio, Texas."

His brows arched. "Via Reno?"

"I needed a…vacation first. Some time to think."

"I know what you mean." His expression became solemn and she believed he did indeed know what she meant.

The champagne arrived and as Reed pulled the bottle from the ice bucket, he grimaced at the tawdry gold label. "I'm not sure how many bubbles it will have, but we'll give it a fair go."

She laughed and, as he popped the cork and the champagne fizzed out of the bottle, she felt happier, lighter and more free than she'd felt in months. Also excited. This handsome Aussie had an unsettling effect on her she hadn't experienced in her twenty-four years. It intrigued her and made her feel a little reckless. She'd never been reckless in her life.

Reed poured two glasses of champagne and handed one to her. When she took it, he held up his glass and clicked it against hers. He seemed to consider his words, and his expression was serious for a moment. But then he smiled. "To Reno and vacations and fun."

Fun took on a whole new meaning when she looked into his eyes. "To all of the above," she agreed, took one sip and then another.

Time seemed to fly by as he asked her about San Francisco, and she told him how she loved the Bay and the fog and everything about the city. He described Sydney and the Opera House and the multicultural life there. After he mentioned that his parents owned a ranch, one glass of champagne became two and then three.

At a lull in their conversation, the band played a ballad and Reed nodded to the dance floor. "Would you like to dance?"

It would be a safe way to feel Reed's arms around her, to get a little closer to him without being forward or too reckless. But as he guided her to the dance floor and the heat of his hand made an arousing impression through the cotton of her dress, she knew she was fooling herself if she thought this was going to be safe. He took her into his arms easily, holding her hand close to his chest. The top button of his shirt was open and she could see blond hairs there, tawny like his hair. He was so male and tall and terrifically sexy, she felt light-headed.

Guessing Reed was about thirty-five and probably very experienced, a question sprang from her heart before she could stop it. "You said you were here last night. Did you dance with many women then?"

His jaw was tantalizingly close to her cheek. "I didn't dance with *any* women then."

As she gazed into his blue eyes, she didn't know why, but she believed him. "What did you do?"

"I listened to the music and drank tequila."

She wondered if he'd had tequila tonight before she arrived. What would he taste like if she kissed him?

Her breath hitched as his arms urged her a little closer. He was so strong and sturdy. While they danced through one song, her breasts grazing his chest, his thighs powerfully guiding her legs, his heat and scent and maleness surrounding her, the night took on a dreamlike quality. There were other cou-

ples all around them, but the world existed for just
the two of them. They didn't even part when the
music stopped…and then started again. It seemed
very natural when Reed rubbed his jaw along her
temple…when his lips brushed her cheek near her
ear…when he lifted her mouth to his. His kiss was
shockingly sensual, and the sensations it created inside her were brand new, seductive and arousing.
She'd *never* felt this way with Winston. This Australian cowboy tasted like champagne and mystery and
something she'd wanted all her life but never found.

Reed restrained desire that was fast getting out of
control. When Mallory had stepped inside the Golden
Spur, he'd wondered if the tequila had gone to his
head. She'd looked like a beautiful angel in that
white dress. When she'd responded to his smile by
coming to his table, his bruised ego had felt much
better.

Not only his ego had felt better. As he'd gotten a
whiff of perfume or shampoo or whatever it was that
smelled like flowers, watched her silky hair slide over
her creamy shoulders, and recognized the intelligence
sparkling in her hazel eyes, he'd wanted her. Their
fingers had brushed as they'd talked; their eyes meeting again and again. His knee had grazed hers more
than once, and he'd asked himself—Did he want her
so much because Stephanie had rejected him? Was
that why he'd invited Mallory to his table? Did fun
mean pleasure?

He'd never treated women as objects and he wasn't
about to start now, certainly not because he was angry or bitter or frustrated. But those feelings had left
as soon as Mallory had sat at his table, and now….

All he wanted to do was to carry her off to his

motel room. As she responded to his kiss, she linked her hands behind his neck, pressed into him, and fervently met his tongue. She was arousing him as much as he hoped he was arousing her. This wasn't his style. He didn't meet women in bars and take them back to his room. Yet a woman's kiss had never aroused him in just this way, making him hungry with a need that could rage out of control. He'd always controlled desire and passion and how much he'd given and how much he'd taken. But kissing this woman named Mallory was an extraordinary experience.

Before he did something indecent on the dance floor, he broke the kiss and rested his forehead against hers. "How about more champagne?"

Her expression was bemused when she leaned away slightly and lifted her chin. "All right. I *am* thirsty."

Curving his arm around her waist, he led her back to their table. This time when he poured the champagne, she clinked her glass against his. "To leaving the past behind."

Looking into her beautiful hazel eyes, he smiled and echoed, "To leaving the past behind."

When Mallory awakened, there was warmth all around her. The sheet grazed her shoulder and something tickled her nose....

The moment she became conscious that she was naked and lying beside a sexy male, her cheek pressed against his chest, she sat bolt upright, leaving at least a foot between her and the man in the king-size bed.

Then she remembered. The bar… dancing…
Reed… She didn't even know his last name!

Appalled and ashamed at behavior that was so unlike her, she put her fingers to her temples, realizing
she had a terrible headache. Not only that, but she
couldn't remember anything past dancing and drinking glass after glass of champagne. When she yanked
the sheet up to her neck, she saw her dress, bra, panties and sandals scattered alongside the bed, and she
groaned. What *had* she done?

Her quick bounce to the headboard must have
awakened Reed. Rising up on one elbow, he slowly
smiled at her. "G'day."

The sight of his tousled hair and rugged face, his
broad shoulders and his bare chest, let alone his
barely covered— "Good day?" she asked, her voice
rising on the last word. "I don't think so." She
scrambled out of bed, taking the sheet with her to
cover herself, then realized she'd left him naked.

Her cheeks flamed with the horror of what she'd
done last night—or what *he'd* done, or what *they'd*
done together. Suddenly the past month of indecision
about Winston, the phone conversation she'd overheard that told her he was a dangerous man, the frantic drive out of San Francisco, leaving her engagement ring and a note to explain to her mother, all
caught up to her.

"How dare you do this to me?" she erupted.

"Do what?" Reed looked just-awakened, rumpled
and terribly sexy. "Wish you a good morning Aus-
sie-style?"

With her gaze firmly planted on his face, she answered, "Take advantage of me like this. How could
you?" Tears threatened. She blinked them away as

she reached to the floor, retrieved her panties, then tried to pull them on from behind the sheet.

Sitting up now, all signs of sleep and amusement gone from his face, Reed's deep voice was firm. "I did *not* take advantage of you."

Draping the sheet across her shoulders, she scrambled into her bra next, but as she fastened the catch, the sheet slipped to the floor. "You certainly did. I told you champagne went to my head and still you kept pouring. *Now* I know why."

When he slid his legs over the side of the bed and stood, looking much too male and intimidating, she grabbed her sundress and backed up a few steps, trying to keep her gaze above his waist.

"You don't know anything," he growled.

Stepping into her dress, she quickly slid her arms under the straps and zipped up the back. "That's possibly quite true. I can't believe I ended up in a motel room with a strange man."

"You didn't think I was strange last night," he argued with the lift of a brow, obviously unconcerned that he was naked.

She slipped into her sandals. "I must have been drunk last night. I've never been drunk before and I've never ever—" Tears caught in her throat and this time she couldn't blink them away as they welled up in her eyes. "I was...I was saving myself for someone special. For someone I was committed to and wanted to spend a lifetime with." She now realized she'd ducked Winston's advances these past few months because she hadn't been committed to him, not in her heart. Finally she'd run because a lifetime with him had seemed unbearable.

If she didn't get out of here, she'd make more of

a fool of herself. The last thing she wanted to do was to let this man see her cry. Her purse lay on the nightstand. Snatching it up, she turned and headed for the door.

"Mallory," Reed called.

But she wouldn't stop. She couldn't stop. Not with tears rolling down her cheeks. Not with her head throbbing and her emotions in so much chaos. She didn't think they'd ever settle down. It wasn't until she closed the door behind her that she realized she didn't even know where she was. But as she raced down two flights of steps and found herself across the street from the Golden Spur Saloon, she got her bearings.

Running down the sidewalk to her motel, she realized Reed's room had been posh compared to the one she'd rented. It had had a sitting area, deep pile carpeting and a nice quality of furnishings. As an interior designer, she recognized quality when she saw it. Unbidden, a vivid picture of a naked Reed popped up before her eyes and she shook her head to clear it. All she wanted to do was to get to San Antonio and her half brother Dawson and put some order back into her life.

The bright sun made Mallory shade her eyes with her hand. As she hurried past the White Dove Wedding Chapel, the cool morning air raised goose bumps on her arms. She remembered feeling chilled last night outside under the stars, and Reed putting his arm around her....

But there wasn't anything else. Maybe in time she would remember her whole sordid night with him. Why had she ever thought dancing and flirting with a stranger wouldn't be dangerous?

When she reached her motel, she breathed a sigh of relief and opened the heavy glass door that led into the lobby. The Sierra Inn wasn't fancy. It had been inexpensive and clean, exactly what she'd been looking for. But instead of spending three days here, she was going to check out early and head for San Antonio.

Fighting off her headache, still feeling off balance and vulnerable because she couldn't remember anything that had happened late last night, she was oblivious to everything around her. How could she not remember a man such as Reed undressing her, touching her—

Someone took hold of her arm in a hard grip and she came to an abrupt halt. Her mind still filled with visions of Reed, she was startled to look up and see— Winston! He was wearing a suit—he always wore a suit—and his grip tightened even more as he said, ''I found you.''

Winston Bentley IV was handsome in a *G.Q.* kind of way. His curly dark brown hair was perfectly parted to the side and his dark brown eyes were angry.

She knew she was in deep trouble, but she told herself she could handle it. ''Winston. What are you doing here?''

He didn't ease his grip. ''More importantly, what are *you* doing here?''

Her conscience told her she owed him an explanation. He had been a diligent suitor, and she'd convinced herself she should marry him because he'd done and said everything right. Her mother and stepfather had approved of him…*more* than approved. But after last night and the attraction she'd felt toward Reed, she decided she'd left San Francisco in the nick of time. "I did both of us an injustice by becoming engaged to you, Winston. I had doubts and I didn't express them."

"Tell me your doubts and I'll put them to rest."

She tried to take the tactful route. "You can't. We're just not right for each other."

"You're very right for me," he said cajolingly. Though his voice was less steely, there was something in it that scared her.

"I can't be, Winston, because I don't really love you."

Releasing her arm, he studied her. "Love? That doesn't enter into this, Mallory. Your marriage to me would be the best thing for both of us. You are exactly what I need in a wife—well-bred, intelligent, poised, sophisticated. I'm not going to let you throw away a future together simply because you have pre-wedding jitters."

She had jitters, all right, but they had nothing to do with her wedding, not anymore. They had to do with that phone conversation she'd overheard. In the iciest voice she could imagine, Winston had told one of his associates, "Do whatever you have to do to get him to sell. Even a little physical persuasion if necessary. Understand?"

She was sure his associate had understood, and so had she. Winston hadn't gotten rich by being honest or nice. Apparently he used force when he felt it was necessary. Looking into his eyes now, she was worried that he wouldn't hesitate to use force on her. But she tried to keep from panicking and reminded herself to stay calm.

Glancing around, she realized the lobby was empty

at the moment and no one even stood as sentinel at the desk. She had to do this on her own. "I didn't have prewedding jitters. I realized I was marrying you because my parents wanted the union more than I did."

"Your parents are very wise."

Nothing she said was sinking in. "I'm not going to marry you, Winston."

"If you need more time, Mallory, I'll give it to you, though it's damn embarrassing to have a wedding set up and my bride run off to God knows where."

"How *did* you find me?"

"Apparently you weren't trying to hide. You used your credit card and your own name. It was very easy."

His voice was so matter-of-fact, it scared her. She suddenly understood that he could buy almost anything he wanted, including information and flunkies who would do his dirty work for him. Yet he had come here for her himself.

Possibly he really had feelings for her. "Winston, I really am sorry. More time isn't going to help. I'm sure marriage isn't in the cards for us."

His cheeks flushed, his eyes glinted, and he clasped her arm again. "Oh, yes, it is, Mallory. And I'm going to tell you all the reasons why it is once we're in the car. Come on."

Attempting to wrench away, she said, "I won't go with you."

Although Winston was only about five-ten, he was strong. She knew he worked out at least three times a week at a men's club that he belonged to with her stepfather. She tried her best to keep her sandals firmly planted on the floor, but at five-five and one hundred and ten pounds, she was no match and he managed to easily pull her along.

"Winston, I said no!" But her words didn't make an impression any more than her wrenches and shoves did. Circling her waist with his arm, he practically carried her to the door. Pushing it open with his knee, he dragged her with him and she was all too aware that she was in a serious situation. A luxury car was parked directly in front of them, and she knew he intended to get her into it one way or another.

"No," she said again. "No!" Realizing he was intent on kidnapping her, she yelled, "Help!" But the streets this time of the morning were dead and there was no one in sight.

Again she tried reason. "Winston, you can't do this. What are you going to do with me once we're back in San Francisco? Keep me locked up?" With a quick glance at him, she immediately realized it wasn't beyond the realm of possibility.

As she squirmed, he somehow managed to hold her tightly while he opened the back car door, and she knew she might not be strong enough to get away. She could be his prisoner—

Fearing her fate was sealed, fearing what Winston would do with her once he got her into his car, she was startled by a familiar deep voice.

"What's going on here?" Reed asked, his expression grim.

"It's none of your business," Winston snapped.

This time Mallory managed to wrench away from him. "I was engaged to him, but I'm not anymore, and I don't want to be, and he's trying to make me go with him." She knew she had no right to ask, but her eyes pleaded with Reed to help her. He wore a tan Stetson this morning with his jeans, boots and blue plaid Western-cut shirt, and she'd never been so happy in her life to see anyone.

Reed pinned Winston with a hard stare. "It seems as if the lady doesn't want to go with you."

"The lady doesn't know what she wants. She's confused."

"Are you confused, Mallory?" Reed asked.

Winston's eyes widened with Reed's use of her first name. Her ex-fiancé had been about to make her out as a whimpering, panicked bride-to-be who didn't know her own mind. She wouldn't let him get away with that. "No, I'm not confused. I do *not* want to marry him, and I'm not going back to San Francisco."

"That's that, then," Reed said with a shrug. "You heard the lady, Mr...."

"Winston Bentley the Fourth, and I might have heard the lady but she doesn't know her own mind. Her stepfather is *the* George Pennington Smythe from San Francisco, and he sent me after her. He's worried about her." Winston leaned forward as if to confide in Reed man-to-man. "She's been on edge, nervous, on tranquilizers. Once I get her home—"

Mallory stepped forward, closer to Reed and away from Winston. "I've never taken a tranquilizer in my life and if I hadn't been sure about not marrying him before this, I certainly would be now."

"Mallory, honey," Winston said engagingly. "We'll talk this all out. If you don't want to live in my penthouse, we'll buy a house somewhere—"

"She's not going anywhere with you, Bentley."

Reed's voice was firm and steady, and Mallory breathed a sigh of relief because this handsome Aussie believed she *did* know her own mind.

Winston's expression was almost a snarl. "Look here, you...whatever your name is."

"Reed Fortune."

"Fortune?" Mallory gasped at the same time as Winston.

"The Texas Fortunes?" Winston asked. "The ones in all the newspapers and tabloids last year?"

"My branch is from Sydney, Australia."

"I don't care who you are or where you're from," Winston retorted. "She's *my* fiancée."

Reed's voice was calm as he reached into the back pocket of his jeans and produced a paper that was folded into quarters. "Not anymore." He unfolded the piece of paper slowly, then handed it to Winston Bentley IV with the announcement, "Mallory and I got married last night."

Two

Mallory's face turned so pale, Reed thought she would faint. He convinced himself that that was the reason he circled her waist and held her close to him. Of course, Winston Bentley IV was another. "There's no point in your sticking around, Bentley. She's *my* wife now."

The angry man looked from one to the other. "Something's not right here. Mallory, tell me you didn't marry this man."

Mallory still looked stunned, and Reed answered for her. "You have the proof in your hands."

After examining the document, Bentley thrust it at Reed. "Don't think this is over. I always get what I want, and Mallory Prescott is the woman I want for my wife."

Last night when she'd signed her name, Reed had wondered if she was related to the Dawson Prescott who worked for Fortune TX, Ltd. But that hadn't been foremost on his mind, and he'd expected there would be time enough for questions and explanations this morning. Now they'd have to wait until he sent Bentley on his way. It was a good thing he'd caught sight of Mallory running down the street as he'd looked out his motel room window. He'd been able to follow her. "I hear bigamy is illegal in the United

States. Since Mallory has a husband, she won't be taking another."

Bentley's face flushed redder. "You haven't heard the end of this."

"I expect not," Reed muttered as he guided Mallory toward the door of the motel.

"Her stepfather won't stand for this," Bentley called after them, then added, "Don't think you can hide from me, Mallory. Because I'll find you."

Reed could feel the shudder that trembled through Mallory, and he only had one thought. He had to protect her.

Once inside the motel lobby, he spotted Bentley still watching them. Leaning close to Mallory, Reed asked, "What room are you in?"

She looked up at him as if she was seeing him for the first time. Her expression was troubled, perplexed and very vulnerable. She still smelled of flowers, and he vividly remembered her curled against him in sleep.

"Your ex-fiancé is still watching us," he murmured in her ear. "Let's go to your room for your things so I can get you out of here."

Without a word she opened her purse and handed him her key. Her room was on the second floor.

As soon as they reached it and Reed closed the door behind them, she turned to face him. "Married? We can't be."

He couldn't believe she didn't remember finishing the bottle of champagne, leaving the Golden Spur, and walking in the star-filled night. He'd wanted her badly. Dancing had primed him and the longer he'd been with her, the more aroused he'd become. Outside she'd shivered and he'd put his arm around her, feeling protective and powerful and everything else a man should feel when he wanted a woman and guessed that that woman wanted him.

Yet something about Mallory had made it impossible for him to simply take her to his room. He'd never done anything so impulsive in his life, but he'd asked her to marry him. Maybe it was Stephanie's rejection that had prompted it. Maybe it was the fact that Mallory was more beautiful to him than any woman he'd ever laid eyes on. Maybe it was because he'd wanted her too badly to let her slip out of his life in the morning. Whatever it had been, it had been sheer craziness, but she'd agreed.

Had the tequila and champagne led him to hail a cab to take them to the courthouse, then return to the White Dove Wedding Chapel a few doors down from his motel? Another question he couldn't answer. It didn't much matter because now they *were* married. Taking the paper out of his pocket again, he handed it to her.

She examined it, studied her signature, then sank onto the bed. "Oh, my heavens," she murmured, looking dumbfounded.

Last night Mallory's flirting and sparkling, desire-filled hazel eyes had made Reed feel ten feet tall. Now her stricken expression made him feel much the same as Stephanie's letter had. "You don't remember any of it?" he asked her.

Gazing up at him, she shook her head. "I never drink. One glass usually makes me fall asleep."

"Yeah, well you had more than one glass," he mumbled. "You don't remember finishing the bottle?"

She sighed, then shook her head again. "Tell me what happened, Reed. I have to know."

She looked mortified, and he couldn't help but sit beside her on the bed, though no part of them touched. That could be entirely too dangerous right now. "We drank. We danced. We kissed. We danced. We drank some more. We started walking to my motel and...I asked you to marry me."

"Why?"

Her surprise was so genuine that he knew he had to be honest with her. "I wanted to have sex with you, but you were so sweet and such a lady, that I guess I didn't feel I could unless I asked you to marry me."

She was silent for a few moments. Then she asked, "So we...slept together?"

"Sleep is *all* we did."

"I don't understand. I thought you said—"

"I said I wanted to have sex with you. But after our visit to the courthouse and the wedding chapel, we came back to my motel room. I went into the bathroom, and when I came out, you had taken off your clothes and crawled into bed and were fast asleep."

"So you just crawled in beside me?"

He shrugged. "That's about it. Look, I knew you'd had too much champagne, and I guess deep down I knew you'd want a divorce in the morning."

"So you didn't take advantage of me," she responded with a relieved look.

"I'm no saint. I guess I hoped that when we awakened, I wouldn't *have* to take advantage of you."

She thought about that for a moment. "Reed, all I can say is thank you for being more than an honorable man last night, as well as for rescuing me this morning.''

"Bentley is dangerous,'' Reed said with certainty.

"I just realized how dangerous,'' Mallory murmured. She looked lost in thought, but then she turned toward him slightly on the bed. "Your name's really 'Fortune'?''

"So my father tells me,'' he said with a smile, glad she wasn't looking quite as shaken or panicked.

"Do you know the Texas Fortunes?''

He nodded. "It's a long story, but Ryan Fortune and my father, Teddy, are long-lost half brothers. Ryan and Dad were just reunited about six months ago at Ryan and Lily's wedding. I'm visiting, getting to know the family, learning about the horse operation here, hoping I can convince my father to modernize back home.''

Mallory shook her head and smiled. "It's a small world. My half brother works for the Fortunes in San Antonio.''

"Would his name be Dawson Prescott?''

"How did you know?''

"You said you were on your way to San Antonio. When I saw your last name, I wondered if you were related to Dawson. I've spent some weekends with him on the Double Crown.''

With Mallory's face turned up to him, her hazel eyes now devoid of fear, Reed found himself as attracted to her as he had been last night. But the situation had gotten complicated and they would have to unravel it piece by piece. Standing, he said, "You'd better get your things together. Bentley might return with reinforcements. I'll call the airport and tell them to get the jet ready.''

"Jet?"

"I flew the company jet up here."

Her back straightening, she pushed her hair behind her ear. "I can pack my things, load up the car and drive to Texas. I don't want to interrupt your plans."

"I think you already have." As soon as he said it, he saw a look in her eyes that he decided was pure determination.

"I left San Francisco to make my own decisions, Reed, and to start a new life in Texas on my own."

"That's going to be a little tough with Bentley on your heels, don't you think? What if you stop for a meal and he pulls the same thing he pulled here? If you drive away from Reno alone, you won't have any protection against him. He'll know our marriage isn't a marriage."

"I don't want to get you mixed up in this."

She was dismissing the idea of their marriage as if it had never happened, and he probably should, too. But he couldn't. Not when Bentley was on her tail. "At least let me deliver you to Dawson safely, then you can decide what you want to do next."

"But my car is here, and I'm going to need it in San Antonio."

"If I can find someone to drive it to Texas for you, will you fly home with me?"

"Only if the driver is reliable and will get my car there in one piece."

"I know someone who can take care of it."

When Reed had first arrived in Reno and looked up Matt Conroy, the owner of the Golden Spur, they'd had a lengthy conversation. Matt had told him he was aiming to visit some relatives in Texas very soon. Maybe now would be a good time if Reed offered to pay his airfare back.

Sensing Mallory had an adventurous streak she was only beginning to discover, he upped the ante. "I could be persuaded to let you sit in the cockpit with me."

She laughed. "That's a bribe, Reed Fortune."

"Yes, it is, Mallory Prescott."

With a smile, she stood and faced him toe to toe. "All right. I'll fly to San Antonio with you, but then I take care of myself."

He'd let her take care of herself, but only if she was out of harm's way while she did it.

While Reed spoke with the men who were buzzing around the jet emblazoned with the Double Crown insignia, Mallory stood inside the airport trying to catch her breath. She couldn't believe she'd married this sexy Australian, and she vowed to herself she'd never touch liquor again. *A little late now that the damage is done,* she thought. Thank goodness Reed was an honorable man. Maybe they could both get out of this thing unscathed.

As she admired his tall, well-built frame, she remembered seeing him naked this morning, and she felt the heat rising inside her again. He wasn't *really* her husband. *Couldn't* be her husband. She didn't know anything about the Australian branch of the Fortunes, but the Texas ones were certainly wealthy. The last thing she wanted was to be involved with another wealthy man. Winston and her stepfather seemed to think women were possessions. She was having none of that ever again. She'd make a life for herself on her own terms.

Reed saw her standing at the window and motioned for her to join him. A stiff breeze almost whipped her sweater from her shoulders as she stepped outside. She'd changed at her motel into mint-green slacks, a silk shirt and matching sweater. She'd only brought along clothes that she'd packed for her honeymoon. She and Winston were supposed to spend the week in Bermuda in a posh hotel that recommended dressing for high tea. When she'd emerged from the bathroom at the motel in this outfit, Reed had given her the once-over but hadn't said anything. She couldn't tell what he was thinking. He'd told her he'd made arrangements for her car, and they should leave for the airport immediately. Both lost in their own thoughts, they hadn't talked much on the drive.

Now Reed asked, "Do you still want to ride up front?"

She nodded.

"Go on up, then," he said. "I'll be ready in a few minutes."

Even she could tell the aircraft was state of the art as she settled in and fastened her seat belt. The instrument panel meant nothing to her. When Reed climbed inside, she gave him a tentative smile. "Do you do much of this?"

"Are you worrying about how experienced I am?"

The glimmer of amusement in his eyes made her blush. She'd bet he was experienced in more than flying an airplane. "Do you fly in Australia?"

"As often as I can. I fly jets now and then on excursions, and we have a twin engine on the Crown Peak."

"The Crown Peak?"

"The name of my family's ranch. Both Ryan and my dad, like all the Fortunes, have a hereditary birthmark in the shape of a crown."

It was on the tip of her tongue to ask if Reed did. She'd tried so hard not to look at his naked body this morning.... Keeping her lips firmly closed to keep herself out of trouble, she stared straight ahead.

After Reed had done everything necessary for takeoff and spoken with the tower, they taxied to the runway, then waited until he received a go-ahead. Looking over at her, he said, "Here we go. Are you nervous?"

She shook her head. "Excited."

With that slip of a smile that made her stomach flip-flop, he focused his attention and they took off.

Leaving the Sierra Nevada behind them, Mallory couldn't help glancing at Reed as well as at the scenery. His hands were large and capable, his movements quick and deft. He'd taken off his Stetson and was wearing a headset. His profile was strong and defined. She might not remember marrying him, but she sure remembered kissing him, drowning in the sensuality of it—

Turning his head, he caught her looking. She quickly looked away.

After a few moments Reed remarked, "I suppose you saw the articles about the Fortunes in the newspapers and tabloids that Bentley referred to."

"About Ryan Fortune's grandson being kidnapped? Or about his fiancée, Lily Cassidy, being accused of murdering the wife he was divorcing? Sophia, I think."

Reed grimaced. "Unfortunately, the Fortunes are

newsworthy without the crises the family has been through.''

''The baby was returned unharmed, wasn't he?''

Reed nodded. ''And Lily was cleared of Sophia's murder.''

''From what I read, Lily and your uncle Ryan knew each other when they were younger, before his two marriages.''

''They were much younger. Did Dawson tell you about the scandals?''

''Some. He said he knew Lily could never murder anyone. He was relieved when Clint Lockhart was arrested for murdering Sophia.''

''Lockhart had revenge on his mind for years. Another dangerous man.''

Mallory knew Reed was referring to Winston. She'd never suspected he'd try to kidnap her.

Reed must have been thinking about what had happened that morning, too, because he asked, ''Did you manage to reach Dawson from the airport?''

''No. I still got his machine, and the Fortune offices are closed on Saturday.''

''Maybe he's at the Double Crown. He has an open invitation to visit anytime he wants. My uncle is like that with people he trusts. But I guess you know that.''

''You mean, because of Dawson?''

Reed nodded.

''He's mentioned going riding at the Double Crown.'' Wishing she knew much more about her half brother, her voice was a bit wistful.

''Are you and Dawson close?'' Reed asked.

''Not as close as I'd like. We have the same father. But Dad left Dawson's mother for mine and created so much bitterness that my mother did everything she could to dissuade contact between us. My dad, on the other hand, tried to bring Dawson and me together now and then. We'd go to Disneyland or have lunch. Dawson used to tell me if I needed him I could call him, so when he was in college, I did. But whenever my mother saw the bill, she had a fit.''

''What about more recently?''

For some reason it seemed natural to talk to Reed about her family. ''My life was as hectic as Dawson's and it was hard to connect. Since I was still living with my mother and stepfather, I tried to keep peace. I should have moved out after college. But I was doing an apprenticeship, which Mother and George were totally against. They didn't like the idea of my working at all. So to calm the waters somewhat, I stayed with them.''

Reed glanced at her briefly. ''What about your father?''

''He died when I was seventeen,'' she said softly. She still missed him desperately. They'd been close and when he'd died, she'd felt cut adrift. Her mother's remarriage a year later hadn't helped.

Giving her a quick look, Reed didn't pursue the conversation any further. After another stretch of silence when the only sound was the hum of the engine, Reed picked up a phone from between their seats and quickly punched in a number. ''I'm going to check to see if Dawson is at the Double Crown.''

When someone answered, Reed asked, ''Rosita, it's Reed. Is Dawson there this weekend?'' After a pause he said, ''I see. Is Zane around? Maybe he can tell me.'' Turning toward Mallory, Reed explained, ''Dawson's not there. But Zane, Ryan's son, works with him at the Fortune offices. He should know what's going on.''

Anxiety tightened Mallory's chest. What if no one knew where Dawson was?

Reed asked his cousin about Dawson's where-abouts and then listened. Finally he responded, ''Are you going to be there for a while? Either I'll call you back or I'll answer your questions after I land. Talk to you soon.'' Putting the phone back on its holder, Reed readjusted his headset, then said matter-of-factly, ''You have a problem.''

''Dawson?'' she asked.

''He's away on business and Zane doesn't expect him back for two weeks. He flew to Europe to check on new investment possibilities. Zane has his itinerary, if you want to call him, but I get the impression that he has meetings scheduled daily for the time he's there. Even if he came back to help you get settled, he'd have to leave again. The way I see it, you have three options.''

''Why do I get the feeling I'm not going to like any of them?'' she murmured.

He gave her a wry look. ''You can go back to San Francisco and forget about this whole adventure.''

''That one's out,'' she responded quickly.

''You could stay at Dawson's place and be a sitting duck if Winston comes calling again.''

''I'm not particularly fond of that one, either.''

''Or finally, we could pretend to have a real marriage and you could stay with me.''

With all that had happened, she didn't think anything Reed could say would shock her, but that came close. Besides the fact that ''pretend'' and ''real'' didn't seem to go together in the same sentence. "Explain '*pretend* to have a real marriage.'"

"We have a marriage certificate. All I have to do is tell Zane to spread the word and everyone will know we're married. I'm staying in a cabin on the Double Crown property. No one has to know what you and I do when we're alone."

"And just what will you and I be doing?" she asked.

"Whatever we want."

"What do *you* want? Why are you willing to do this?"

He answered without hesitating. "I feel responsible. I'm the one who got you drunk. I'm the one who suggested we get married. Obviously you didn't have all your wits about you or you'd remember it. I'm not in the habit of throwing women to the wolves. That's what I'd be doing if I let you stay alone somewhere else. Ryan has twenty-four hour patrol guards on the ranch because of security concerns in the past, and the cabin has reliable locks. You would be safe there."

Just thinking about staying in a cabin with Reed—

"The cabin has a bedroom, and it has a living room. You can take the bedroom, and I'll sleep on the fold-out sofa in the living room. You already know your virtue is safe with me if you want to keep it."

"I *have* to keep it. I mean… If we want to get this marriage annulled, nothing can happen."

"Nothing *has* to happen," Reed told her gruffly. "When Dawson gets back, you can decide what you're going to do next."

"You're not going to tell anybody the truth?"

"We got married, Mallory. That *is* the truth." His jaw became set.

As if she were reliving it, she remembered Winston's grip on her arm. She remembered his arms locking her against him, and him practically carrying her to his car. Unless she learned self-defense in a very short amount of time, all that could easily happen again. In contrast to the panicked feeling she experienced whenever she thought about Winston, she could also remember the safe feeling waking up snuggled against Reed.

The devil or the deep blue sea, she thought wryly. She guessed she'd take the plunge into the deep blue sea. "All right. We'll pretend we're married until Dawson gets back. But I'm not your responsibility, Reed. I want you to know that. I don't want to be anybody's responsibility but my own anymore."

He studied her for a prolonged moment and then picked up the phone again.

When they landed, everyone at the Double Crown would know that they were married.

Winston Bentley IV was an intelligent man who knew he'd been stalled for the moment. He'd made himself rich by always staying one step ahead of his opponent. This situation was no different. He boarded a flight to San Francisco. Once settled in first class, he phoned the man who always got him the information he needed, when he needed it.

"I want everything you can get me on Reed Fortune," he snapped. "He's from Australia, connected to the Fortunes in Texas. I want to know why he's here, how long he's going to be here, and exactly where he's staying. Give me everything he's done in

the past six months. No, make it a year. I expect to
hear something from you by the time I land.''

Not comfortable with competition in any form,
Winston usually decimated it. Reed Fortune was no
different than rival developers who got in his way or
property owners who wouldn't sell. The right information, money, as well as selective arm-twisting
worked wonders.

After landing in San Francisco, Winston hailed a
taxi and headed toward George Pennington Smythe's
address. When his cell phone rang, he took it out of
his pocket and listened carefully. In a few minutes
he had the information he needed. Tucking the phone
back into his suitcoat, a small smile crossed his lips.
This wasn't going to be too difficult. Mallory Prescott
was used to luxury. The Fortunes might have money,
but Reed Fortune seldom acted as if he did. Apparently, he worked hard training horses and running a
ranch with his family. But the important tidbit his
source had discovered was an engagement announcement that had appeared in a Sydney newspaper. It
had claimed that while Reed Fortune and Stephanie
Milton hadn't yet set a date, they were planning to
marry sometime in the new year.

Winston deduced that nothing fit. Mallory Prescott
was *not* used to ranch life. She also wasn't an impulsive woman. She wouldn't decide to marry a man
in a day's time. Winston knew everyone she'd seen
and met because he'd had her investigated and had
kept close tabs on her since they'd become engaged.
She hadn't known Reed Fortune before yesterday. He
was sure of it.

When Winston rang the doorbell of George Pennington Smythe's mansion, a maid let him inside. A

few minutes later George met him in the parlor. "Have you found Mallory?"

Winston smiled reassuringly. "I certainly did. Where's Gloria? She needs to hear this."

"She's on the phone, still canceling arrangements and trying to explain to everyone why the wedding didn't take place. I'm so embarrassed about this, Winston. Mallory is usually so reliable, so steady."

Mallory's mother Gloria came rushing in before Winston could comment. "Oh, Winston. Did you find her? Is she all right? That note with her engagement ring didn't tell me anything except that she was going away to think. I don't know why she has to think when she's about to marry you."

Winston studied Gloria Pennington Smythe. Blond, brown eyes, ivory complexion, she was very attractive for a woman her age, which had to be around forty-five. But she looked thirty-five if a day. He'd had affairs with women ten years older than himself before, and they'd been quite satisfactory. He might have made a move on Gloria if he hadn't met Mallory and realized as an investment banker with good contacts, George could be a valuable in-law to have. They'd already pulled off a few successful deals together, legitimate by-the-book deals. George didn't know his future son-in-law operated any other way.

Winston had set his sights on Mallory and had been quite successful about it until she'd run away. "I found her, Gloria, but there's a problem."

"What kind of problem?" George asked.

"I think the stress of working and of planning the wedding have made her unbalanced. I think she's afraid she'll disappoint me in some way. Instead of asking me for more time, she's done something foolish."

"What has she done?" Gloria asked, looking as if she were near tears.

"She married a stranger last night."

"You aren't serious!" both her parents said at once.

"I'm very serious. And not just any stranger. His name is Reed Fortune, nephew of Ryan Fortune of Texas."

"The family that's always in the news?" Gloria asked.

"That's the one."

"What are we going to do?" George wanted to know. "I suppose I could drive down there and get her...."

Winston shook his head. "I think that would be a mistake right now. We don't want to do anything that might make her act even more foolishly and do something like bolt back to Australia with this man."

"Australia!" Gloria gasped.

"Apparently he's from the Australian branch of the Fortune family." Winston paused for a moment. "I don't think she wanted to marry him. She did it to get out of marrying me. Soon enough she'll discover it was a mistake. You've raised your daughter well, Gloria, with certain advantages. She'll miss those."

"But the Fortunes are rich," George exclaimed.

"The Fortunes might be, but Reed Fortune is another matter. Right now he's living in a cabin on the property of the Double Crown. Can you imagine Mallory cooped up in two or three rooms with a man she doesn't really know?"

He smiled, thinking about it. ''We just have to give her a little bit of time to come to her senses, and I think with a little persuasion that will happen. Gloria, I think she'll need an understanding ear. In a couple of hours she'll be there and wonder what she's gotten herself into. If you give her a call, you can tell her how much we all care about her. It will set her thinking in the right direction.''

Gloria smiled at Winston. ''Mallory doesn't know how lucky she is to have you, how fortunate she is to have a man who understands her.''

Winston understood Mallory, all right. He understood that he wanted her for his wife, and she would become his wife no matter what he had to do. But before he pulled out all the stops, he'd give her a little time to let her realize how foolish she'd been and how much better off she would be with him.

All it would take was time. He had plenty of that, unlike Reed Fortune who would be going back to Australia eventually.

Soon, if Winston had anything to say about it.

Three

When Reed brought the jet in for a landing on the Double Crown's airstrip, the touchdown was smooth and faultless. He and Mallory disembarked from the aircraft and descended the steps. Hot Texas air swept against Mallory's face, and she shed her sweater. As she draped it over her arm, a tall, solidly built man wearing a white Stetson approached them from the metal hangar. He looked to be in his fifties, with dark brown hair, dark eyes and deeply tanned skin.

He approached Reed and Mallory with a smile and extended his hand to Reed. "Congratulations, boy. Zane told us the good news. A little unexpected, especially since you just—"

Reed took hold of the older man's hand and hooked his arm around Mallory's shoulders. "Let me introduce you to my wife. Mallory, this is my uncle, Ryan Fortune. Ryan, this is Dawson's sister. Small world, isn't it?"

"Zane mentioned that. Fate just happened to bring you two to the Golden Spur at the same time. Just like it brought me and Lily back together again." Ryan looked down at Mallory. "My wife's out shopping or she'd be here to welcome you yourself. Do you want to come up to the house or would you rather get settled in?"

Mallory was all too aware of Reed's arm around

her, its weight and its heat. He was hard and strong. She just had to remember she was doing this only until Dawson returned. "I'd love to, Mr. Fortune, but—"

"Please call me Ryan. We don't stand on formality here. I understand if you need to rest before meeting the rest of the family," Ryan said with a smile. Then he clapped Reed on the shoulder. "Something's missing here, boy."

Mallory had no idea what Ryan Fortune was referring to and she looked up at Reed, but he seemed just as perplexed as she was.

"You two aren't wearing wedding rings."

Looking chagrined, Reed responded, "We're going to take care of that in the next few hours. We did everything so suddenly, the rings got lost in the shuffle."

With a knowing look, Ryan laughed. "I'd imagine so. Some short honeymoon you had."

Mallory could feel herself blushing and knew it wasn't the Texas heat.

"C'mon." Ryan motioned toward his Cherokee. "Hank will load up your luggage in the back and I'll give you a ride to your cabin. I had Rosita stock the refrigerator and cupboards for you. I hope that's all right."

Reed guided Mallory toward the Jeep. "You didn't have to do that, sir."

"My pleasure. Just consider it a preliminary wedding present. Mallory, you can do anything you want to the cabin. Make it feel like home. I guess it will be the only one you'll have until the two of you go back to Australia."

Australia.

Yes, she knew Reed had come from Australia, but she had no idea when he was going back. It didn't matter. As soon as Dawson returned, she could make some real plans and this episode with Reed would be just a memory.

Mallory and Reed rode in the back as Ryan gave Mallory a brief tour of his estate. When he pointed to the ranch house he shared with Lily, Mallory saw that it was huge. It was an adobe structure with sand-colored walls surrounded by a sandstone wall. He told Mallory the arched entryway and wrought-iron gate led into an inner courtyard. As the generations of families grew, they had added another wing. The house was about half a mile from the barn and out-buildings.

They passed another ranch-style house, a miniature of the larger one. Ryan explained his son Dallas and wife Maggie lived there. As they rode past fences and gently rolling land, Ryan also pointed out where his sister-in-law Mary Ellen and her husband Sam lived. They were away on vacation but would be home for the Double Crown's summer barbecue next weekend. After another mile or so, they passed Ruben and Rosita Perez's ranch-style home, and he explained that Rosita was his housekeeper. Her husband Ruben helped with the horses, or grounds, or wherever he was needed. Their son Cruz now had his own cabin and horse-breeding business at a ranch near his parents' home.

When Mallory thought about a cabin, she thought of logs and rough-hewn beams and plank flooring. But here a cabin took on a different description. They pulled up in front of an adobe with a red-tiled slanted roof. A curving stone walkway led to the door, which had a wooden screen on the outside. The lawn area was small, and a variety of shrubs and blooming plants created an engaging effect. She recognized crepe myrtle, daylilies and a rosebush climbing an arbor along the side of the adobe.

"This is charming," she said.

Both men got out of the car. Ryan helped Reed with the luggage but at the door, tipped his hat to Mallory. "I'll leave you two alone for now, but if you want company, come on up to the house."

Reed unlocked the door and let Mallory precede him over the threshold. Inside, she did find plank hardwood flooring, but the walls were plaster and a fan revolved in the living room's high ceiling. Considering the 90-degree temperature outside, the inside of the adobe was fairly comfortable as a breeze blew in the high, transom-like windows. There was a kitchen to the right, just large enough for the oven, refrigerator, sink and a few cabinets. To the left, Mallory noticed an archway and could see the corner of a bed covered by a tan spread. The fold-out sofa Reed had mentioned was forest green and looked new, as did the pine coffee table, end tables and small dining table flanked by two straight-backed chairs. Only the high-backed wooden rocker by the small fireplace looked as if it might have seen generations of use. A beautiful lamp with a bronze, bucking bronc base sat near the sofa.

Reed hung his hat on a rack by the door. "Lily had ordered new furniture for the place before I arrived. She told me she'd send a decorator in to spruce it up a little, but I said it wasn't necessary."

"Did someone live here before you?" Mallory asked.

"Clint Lockhart lived here for years when he worked on the Double Crown until he was sent to prison. It's hard to believe during all that time he hated the Fortunes. Especially since Ryan was his brother-in-law. Both of his sisters married Fortune men."

"Why did he hate them so much?" Mallory asked, stepping deeper into the room, automatically thinking about what she could do to the place to liven it up.

"He believed Ryan's father, Kingston Fortune, stole his father's land. Ryan says the truth was, Clint's father would have gone bankrupt if Kingston hadn't bought him out. Anyway, after Clint went to prison, Ryan had all the old furniture taken out."

The room wasn't very big and with Reed only about two feet away, she realized that if they weren't careful, they would be bumping into each other. Remembering how perfectly their bodies had fit together while they'd danced, she walked toward the small bedroom, trying to put that detail out of her mind.

Next to a closet there was a small dresser and a washstand with a mirror. Reed brought her suitcase and cosmetics case into the room and set them on the double bed.

"Are you sure about me taking the bedroom?" she asked.

His eyes seemed to turn a crystalline blue as his gaze held hers. "I'm sure. I'll only bother you when I have to get in and out of the drawers or the closet. Or to shower," he said, nodding to the small bathroom.

Its door was half closed and, unbidden, she pictured Reed in the shower...naked— Swallowing hard, she laid her purse on the coffee table and draped her sweater over the arm of the rocker.

When the phone rang, Reed crossed to the kitchen in three long strides and took the receiver from the wall. Arching his brow, he held it out to Mallory. "It's your mother. Bentley's a fast worker."

Apparently Winston had gone straight home to San Francisco and to her parents. "Mother?"

"Mallory, darling. Are you all right?"

"Mother, I'm fine. I don't know what Winston told you, but he tried to kidnap me."

"Oh, darling. He was right. Working and getting ready for the wedding have just been too much for you."

"Mother, he tried to force me into his car—"

"Honey, Winston can be forceful at times, I know. He only wants what's best for you, just as your step-father and I do. I can't believe you married some stranger. George says we can get it annulled, and I'm sure we can. If you just come home, we'll straighten this all out."

"Mother, he not only tried to kidnap me. I heard him talking to someone on the phone before I left. You and George don't understand how he does business. He's dangerous."

"Now, Mallory. Winston's business isn't any of your concern…or mine. I'm sure you misunderstood whatever you heard. And you're overreacting. If you would just come home…"

Mallory now realized Winston had shown all of them only what he'd wanted them to see for the past six months. Even now he'd convinced her parents that he wanted what was best for her, and he had them completely buffaloed. "I'm not coming home."

"But you must. What will you do there? You can't stay with that man. Someone you don't even know."

Apparently she hadn't known Winston, yet she'd planned to marry him! Instead of getting into an argument with her mother about her quick marriage, she ventured into territory that had never been safe. "Dawson is here, Mother."

There was silence on the other end of the line. "You know how I feel about him and his mother," Gloria finally responded.

"Yes, I know. But that's not fair to me and Dawson. Maybe we'll really get to know each other now that I'm here."

After another pause Gloria Pennington Smythe asked, "Isn't there anything I can say that will put you on a plane back home to us?"

"No, Mother. I'm sorry, but I can't come home."

"You just need a little time to see the foolishness of this. Your life is here. Your future is here." When Mallory didn't react, Gloria sighed. "All right, darling. In a few days I'll call again to see how you are. Promise me you'll call me if you need me."

That was the whole problem. She didn't want to need anyone. "I'll check in every once in a while to let you know I'm perfectly fine." She loved her mother and she didn't want her to worry. It was just so frustrating sometimes talking to her.

"This man...Winston says he's a Fortune."

"Mother, please try not to worry."

"Darling, I've worried since the day you were born. Specifically about something like this. A man taking advantage of who you are, what you'll have someday. Your inheritance will make you a wealthy woman."

Yes, and Winston knew that. "Mother, I can assure you Reed isn't interested in my money." When she looked up at him, their eyes met and she could see the desire glowing there—the same desire that had glowed all last evening. Reed Fortune was interested in something else entirely.

After reassuring her mother another time or two, Mallory finally hung up.

"Is Bentley giving them the impression you're unbalanced?"

"That about sums it up. Mother won't listen to me. But then, she and George aren't very good at listening." Mallory was suddenly very tired, and her headache had returned. With Reed standing close, her heart was beating much too fast.

He must have seen her fatigue because he said, "Why don't you get settled in, take a shower and rest. I have a few calls to make, and then I'll read for a while."

"Does that mean you're going to stand guard over me? I don't need or want a baby-sitter, Reed." Already she was much too aware of him in the confined space of the cabin. She had to admit to herself she wanted to feel his lips on hers again and that could only lead to trouble.

"If this charade is going to work," she continued, "We've got to give each other some space. You said there's a twenty-four hour patrol and there are reliable locks on the doors. If you have something else to do this afternoon, please go do it. I'll be fine here."

He studied her for a few moments, apparently realizing she'd only agree to pretend to be married if she could keep her independence. "The number for the main house is programmed into the phone. Just press M1. Someone's always there. I need to check on the horses over at the barn. I won't be gone long.''

''A shower and a nap sound like a good idea. Take your time.'' She gave him a tentative smile. With him out of the cabin, maybe she could relax.

A few minutes later she heard the low murmur of Reed's voice on the phone as she unpacked her robe and took it into the bathroom. After her shower, she found that Reed had left. Although she dressed in knit shorts and tank top, she couldn't resist the allure of the bed. She didn't know how long she'd been sleeping when she heard the door to the adobe open and she sat up.

Reed peeked into the bedroom with a smile. ''I have something for you.''

Her stomach growled and she realized she hadn't eaten since sometime on the road yesterday. Maybe he'd brought food. Sliding her legs over the side of the bed, she sat on the edge. ''What?'' she asked.

He took a box from his pocket—a black velvet box—and when he opened it, she saw two gold wedding bands.

The shock of what she'd done hit her again. ''Where did *they* come from?''

''I called the jeweler before I left, the one Ryan uses. He came out to the house and I picked these out. What do you think? Will they suit our purposes?''

Suddenly the lack of control of her life, of what Winston had told her parents, of what her parents thought of the situation with Reed, of knowing she'd be living with this man in very close quarters, made her respond, "If you cared what I thought, you would have let me pick them out with you."

"Pick them out?"

"I mean… You could have at least consulted me. Don't think you'll be making all the decisions while I'm here and I'll follow blindly along."

Reed's face hardened. "I thought you were tired. I thought this was something I could deal with and we'd get it over with."

"Wedding bands shouldn't be something you just get over with!" Then she realized how thoroughly ridiculous that sounded when they were married in name only. But she couldn't take it back and she couldn't back down. Not if she was going to start her own life. Not if she was going to stand on her own two feet.

"Fine. It's done now," he said, tossing the box to the center of the bed. "I'm going back to the barn."

"I might not be here when you get back."

"Mallory—"

"I just want to take a walk and explore a bit. I need some freedom."

"Just because Bentley's in San Francisco doesn't mean you're safe. Freedom won't mean much if he has someone kidnap you."

"Are you trying to scare me?"

Reed ran his hand up and down the back of his neck. "No. I'm telling you to be realistic and to stay close to the cabin. Even Ryan's security may not be foolproof."

"All right," she conceded with a sigh. "I'll stay in the cabin while you're gone."

He looked as if he was debating whether or not he should leave her alone.

"Go back to the barn, if you want. I don't need a watchdog, Reed."

His gaze dropped to the box on the bed, and she tried again to remember marrying him. But she couldn't.

"I'll see you later," he said briskly as he turned and left the bedroom and then the cabin.

Tears pricked in Mallory's eyes. Apparently Reed could be as high-handed as Winston—making arrangements, not consulting her, having a jeweler at his disposal.

What had she done?

Run away from Winston Bentley IV only to marry a man who was just like him?

Usually being around horses settled Reed and soothed him into the rhythm of nature and animals and the land. But the past twenty-four hours had been so extraordinarily different…even the time he'd spent with the horses hadn't settled his thoughts.

As he drove the blue pickup past Rosita and Ruben's house, he realized Mallory was a brand of woman he didn't know. Vulnerable and needing his protection one minute, rebellious and independent the next, she surprised him constantly. Stephanie had been docile, mellow, nondistracting to be around. With Mallory all of his senses were distracted, as well as his thoughts. He should tell her about Stephanie, but the time just hadn't seemed right, not with everything else that had been going on.

This business with the rings…. Was Mallory simply upset he hadn't consulted her? Or was she feeling trapped in a situation not entirely of her own making?

At the cabin, he pulled the pickup onto the gravel

lane beside the adobe and got out. But as he slammed the door he smelled something burning and saw smoke puffing out the side window in the kitchen. When he raced inside, the acrid smell was even stronger and he found Mallory at the stove with two burned skillets. She coughed and tried to fan more smoke out the window.

Reed took a quick look around to make sure nothing was still burning before he pushed open wider the kitchen window, which was larger than the transom windows throughout the rest of the cabin.

"I was trying to cook us supper," she said in explanation. "I found chicken legs in the refrigerator, and I thought I'd make a stir-fry with the frozen vegetables."

The heat from the stove along with the heat of the afternoon had built up inside. Going to the burners on the stove, he poked at the chicken legs that were burned on the outside and obviously not done on the inside. The vegetables in the second frying pan hadn't fared much better. Anyone who would try to fry chicken without a coating or stir-fry frozen vegetables didn't—

He looked at Mallory, her bangs damp against her forehead, her cheeks flushed, her knit top splattered with everything she'd tried to make. "You don't know how to cook, do you?"

"I, uh..." Pulling herself up to her full five foot five inches, she answered him. "No, I don't. But that doesn't mean I can't try."

He couldn't keep a smile from his lips. "At this rate, we're going to waste an awful lot of food until you learn." He'd meant to tease her, but the expression on her face said she hadn't taken it as a joke.

"I just wanted to make dinner. We haven't eaten all day, and I knew you'd probably be hungry."

He was suddenly very hungry but not for food, and the fact that he wanted her in this smoke-filled kitchen with the heat beading his forehead made him realize his good sense was farther away than Australia. "The day ran away from us."

"Not only the day," she said, shaking her head. "I feel as if my whole life has."

The confusion in her voice led him to reach out and touch her hair. It was so silky. She was so very beautiful, and she was his wife. She stood perfectly still as he tucked her hair behind her ear, then couldn't resist setting his mouth on hers. The moment lips touched lips, fiery desire escalated inside of him.

His tongue played with hers until suddenly she pushed away. "We can't do this, Reed. Everything is complicated enough!"

He was just beginning to realize *how* complicated. Stepping away from her, he willed his pulse to slow. "Why don't you go get cleaned up? I'll put something together out here."

She hesitated. "But I should help—"

"Mallory, there's a time to help and there's a time to just let someone else do it."

Not looking happy with either kissing him or his philosophy, she turned away from him and went to the bedroom.

Damn, he hadn't wanted to upset her, but he didn't want to bump elbows and other parts with her in this small kitchen, either. He couldn't do that without wanting to kiss her again. Without wanting—

He swore and opened the refrigerator.

He didn't see Mallory again until he'd stirred up

a concoction of ground beef and beans and tomato sauce with a few spices thrown in and steamed another bag of frozen vegetables. Grabbing a bag of tortilla chips from a cupboard, he poured them into a bowl.

As she came around the corner from the living room, she said, "It smells good." She'd changed into a pair of light blue shorts and a pretty matching top with a square neck that showed a lot of her creamy skin.

"Did you bring three changes of clothes for each day?" he asked, noting again their fine quality, guessing she'd packed for a honeymoon. As she frowned and would have turned away, he caught her arm. "Mallory, wait. I think we need to clear the air."

"It's clear," she said wryly, obviously speaking of the smoke that had filled the adobe earlier.

Ignoring her remark, he gazed down at her, controlling the urge to pull her into his arms. "We've been thrust into this living-together arrangement without really knowing each other. I'm used to living with four brothers and a sister, joking and poking fun most of the time. Obviously that doesn't work with you."

After a moment when she studied him, she said softly, "You weren't like that last night."

Releasing her arm, he let out a long breath. "Last night was…last night. Today we have to be reasonable and figure out what works. There's a patio area out back. Let's take our supper out there and eat it. It will be cooler."

She didn't respond, but then nodded and moved away, picking up the bowl of tortilla chips.

A red Spanish oak and a Mexican sycamore formed a natural canopy over a square area, hard-scaped with crushed stone, at the back of the adobe. The wrought-iron table for two sat in the center and a wrought-iron bench graced the side.

After they were both seated, Reed asked, "So, you're an only child?"

She took a sip of water, then set her glass by her plate. "I always wanted brothers and sisters, and that's why it was so difficult when my mother kept Dawson and me apart."

"But your dad apparently understood." He remembered what she'd told him on the plane about her father bringing her and her half brother together.

"Yes, he did understand. But he was a cardiac surgeon and never home very much. Don't get me wrong, I'm not complaining. I had a terrific child-hood and went to the best schools. Even after Mother married George..." Mallory gave a little shrug. "My stepfather cares about me in his own way. It's just that he's a different kind of man than my father was."

"He wants you to marry Winston?"

"For my own good. You see, he doesn't think I *know* my own good."

Reed couldn't help but smile.

After she dug into her food for a while, she looked up at him. "This is terrific."

"Don't sound so surprised."

"You were right, you know, about me and cook-ing. I never have. We always had a housekeeper who did that." Then she smiled at him with an expression that was as bright as the sun. "But now I can learn, and before I try it again, I'll buy a cookbook. Where did you learn?"

Thinking of the Crown Peak Ranch and the way he'd grown up, he was thankful. "My mother taught all of us. She insists men have to take care of themselves in the kitchen as well as other places."

Mallory smiled. "A very liberated female."

He laughed. "I think you'd like my mother." And for some inexplicable reason, it occurred to him that his mother would like Mallory.

When Mallory asked about his family's ranch, he told her about the Australian stock horses that they raised, claiming that their operation was much smaller than the Double Crown's, but just as fine. The Crown Peak was well respected in New South Wales and surrounding states. At her interested questions, he revealed he'd earned a bachelor's degree in animal sciences from the University of Adelaide.

"You said your father and Ryan were recently reunited. What happened that they were separated?"

"It's a long story," he warned.

"I think my schedule is clear for tonight," she teased.

She *did* have a sense of humor, and he smiled, thinking he'd like to discover all of Mallory Prescott's facets. But keeping his mind on her question, he remembered the saga and began, "My father lost his mother when she died of pneumonia. His father, Kingston Fortune, was overseas fighting in World War Two. There was bad blood between Kingston and my mother's father, Josiah Talbot. He was a religious zealot and believed that Kingston had stolen his innocent daughter. The couple had eloped and moved away because of Josiah." Reed pushed his plate back. "Have I confused you yet?"

Smiling, she shook her head.

Reed propped an arm on the table. "Kingston was overseas when his wife took ill. A well-meaning friend found papers with Josiah Talbot's name and address, and contacted him. When his daughter died, he took the baby—who was my father—so Kingston would never be able to find him. Josiah's church had a mission outside of Sydney. He booked passage on a ship, told my father that Kingston was dead and now he was a Talbot."

"Josiah Talbot sounds like a terrible man—renouncing your father's birthright."

"He *was* terrible. When my father was twelve, he went to work on a sheep station and fell in love with the family's daughter. He learned he had an affinity for horses, and tended the farm's stable. Josiah died when Dad was seventeen, leaving him his birth certificate with his real name—Theodore Kingston Fortune. My dad did some searching into my grandfather's background, longing to find any family he might still have. But he never had the funds to travel here. Once he fell in love, he didn't want to leave my mother. But he did take back the Fortune name before they married."

"So how did he and Ryan finally reunite?"

"My mom knew Dad's dream to come to the U.S. someday and she planned to give him a trip on their fortieth wedding anniversary. Then she heard about the Fortune child who was kidnapped and returned to Ryan Fortune, the son of legendary rancher Kingston Fortune. The newscaster mentioned the kidnapping of Kingston's first son in 1942 and the crown birthmark, as well. Mom and Dad packed their bags and arrived at the Double Crown about six months ago, just in time to see Ryan and Lily became husband and wife.''

"What a terribly sad, yet wonderful story, too!"

Footsteps along the side of the cabin forestalled further comment. Reed recognized their visitor immediately. "Zane, come meet Mallory."

His cousin came over to the table and shook her hand. "It's good to meet you. I was over at Cruz's place, and Dad called."

"Is something wrong?" Reed asked, seeing something in Zane's expression.

"Dad wouldn't say, but he wants all of us up at the house as soon as we can get there. I told him I'd stop here on my way back and tell you. Mallory, he'd like you to come, too. I guess we're going to initiate you into the family in grand style." As his gaze swept the table and the remains of their meal, he added, "I'm sorry I had to interrupt your first night here together."

"Oh, it's all right," Mallory said quickly.

Zane gave Reed a probing look. "How did your parents take the news of your wedding?"

Reed answered, "I haven't told them yet."

"I bet they'll be surprised," Zane remarked. "Are you going to let Stephanie know?"

"There's no need for that," Reed said stiffly, wishing Zane hadn't brought up the subject of his ex-fiancée. Not yet.

Zane's gaze narrowed, and he must have realized he might have stepped into taboo territory. "Well, I'll see you at the house in a little while, then." With a wave of his hand, he left them alone again.

After Zane had rounded the corner, Mallory asked Reed, "Is Stephanie your sister?"

"No. Matilda is my sister. Stephanie is…*was* my fiancée."

"Your fiancée? You mean, you were engaged when you married me?" She sounded disappointed, hurt and dismayed.

"No," he said firmly. There was no easy way to say it. "Last week she broke it off."

Mallory's hazel eyes grew wider. "When last week?"

"The day before I left for Reno."

There was silence for a few moments until Mallory decided, "You went to Reno to nurse a broken heart."

"I went to Reno for a vacation," he said gruffly.

"*That's* why you were drinking tequila and listening to music and not dancing."

"Mallory—"

She continued. "And in a fit of pique, because you felt you had something to prove, you asked me to marry you."

"You're twisting this into something it's not."

"Tell me I'm wrong."

The problem was, he couldn't tell her she was completely off the mark. Yes, he had invited her to his table because he'd had something to prove. However, somehow during the evening, proving had gotten lost in something else entirely. But his silence was Mallory's answer.

"Now I understand," she said. "You got married to get back at a fiancée who hurt you, and I got married because I was too drunk to care. We both should have our heads examined! Sex, payback, confusion.

It doesn't paint a very pretty picture.'' Standing, she took her plate and glass and followed the path under the rose arbor, disappearing from sight.

They had been getting on so well before Zane's arrival, but Reed was sure Mallory would keep even more distance between them now. He'd felt the wall go up higher and thicker than the sturdiest fortress when she'd learned about Stephanie. Standing, he picked up his plate and glass and went inside.

Mallory was rinsing a dish in the sink.

Setting his on the small counter, he said, ''We should wear the wedding rings tonight.''

After a brief silence she murmured, ''I'll get them,'' and avoided his gaze as she dried her hands.

Meeting her in the living room, he watched her open the box. When she took out the smaller ring and put it on her finger, he had the strangest desire to stop her, to do it himself. But that would be ridiculous. Taking the box from her, he put the larger band on his finger. ''Are you ready?''

When he gazed down at her, she looked troubled. ''Maybe I shouldn't go. It's not as if I'm family.''

''If you don't come along, everyone will think something is wrong.''

''And we have to play a happily married couple,'' she said as if it was a death sentence.

''At least until Dawson returns.''

Her troubled expression made him want to take her into his arms and assure her everything would be all right. But she wouldn't let him get close. Not now.

During their short drive to Ryan Fortune's house, Mallory made sure she kept a good foot between her and Reed. It wasn't far, but the silence made it seem like miles away. She couldn't help but wonder what

Reed's fiancée—*ex-fiancée,* she reminded herself, looked like and sounded like. She should have realized a man didn't marry on a whim, and from what she knew of Reed Fortune already, she guessed everything he did had a purpose. She had no right to be upset that he was probably still in love with his fiancée. She was as much to blame for this fiasco as he was. Still...it had been flattering to think that desire and his sense of honor had led them to the courthouse. Now she knew better. Winston had had his ulterior motives, and Reed had had his. That knowledge made her doubt her judgment about men in general.

Reed parked in front of a garden that held masses of large purple sage plants and ornamental grasses in hues of green and blue. She was out of the truck before he could come around to her door. They walked side by side through the arched entryway and open wrought-iron gate. Along the curving stone walkway, the fragrance of roses drifted by, and Mallory scanned the outer courtyard with its paloverde, ornamental grasses, native plants and rocks arranged in what looked like a miniature arroyo. Flowering vines—jasmine, she thought—also perfumed the area as they mounted the adobe steps that led up to the large antique wooden door and covered entryway.

An older woman opened the door. Her dark hair, pulled back into a bun, had one white streak. She was pleasantly plump and her gathered gauzy skirt, which swept to her ankles, increased the effect. She wore a smile as she pulled Reed to her for a tight hug. "Congratulations. I heard all about this whirlwind marriage. Let me meet your special lady."

When she finally let Reed go, he smiled down at

her. ''Rosita Perez, meet Mallory Prescott Fortune. Mallory, Rosita is much more than a housekeeper here. She's also Cruz Perez's mother. I'm working with him at his ranch as well as at the Double Crown. The Perez's are our closest neighbors.''

Mallory intended to extend her hand, but Rosita caught her in a huge bear hug, too. ''Welcome to the family.'' Over Mallory's shoulder she said to Reed, ''She's a beauty.''

Mallory wasn't used to open displays of affection, but found she liked it and this woman who treated Reed as if he were a son.

Keeping her arm around Mallory, Rosita led her inside. The foyer opened up into a great room with a high-beamed ceiling. There was a large open hearth on one wall and curved wooden framed-glass doors at the other end of the room, which Mallory guessed opened up to another courtyard. Through an archway, she could see the dining room. Large leather couches and comfortable chairs in groupings in the living room looked inviting. A huge painted armoire and Western-style pieces, including antler lights and Native American prints, gave the room a warm ambience.

Rosita took Mallory straight to a strikingly beautiful woman standing next to Ryan Fortune. She had high cheekbones, huge dark eyes, an aquiline nose, and her shiny dark hair was worn in a twist at the back of her head. ''Lily, this is Mallory Prescott, Reed's new wife,'' Rosita said. ''Mallory, this is Mrs. Ryan Fortune.''

Mallory extended her hand. ''It's good to meet you.''

The elegant woman wearing a red dress with ge-

ometric designs on the shoulders extended her hand.
"Please, call me Lily. And congratulations."

Reed curved his arm around Mallory's waist and
she stiffened, but then she consciously relaxed knowing she was a partner in this charade. "Thank you."

Reed glanced at Ryan, who was speaking to a tall,
tanned man. From the resemblance between the two
men, Mallory guessed he was one of Ryan's sons.
Reed asked Lily, "Is everything all right?"

Lily shook her head. "I'm afraid not." She took
her husband's elbow. "Ryan, I think everyone's here
now."

Ryan nodded at Reed and Mallory but didn't smile.
"Everyone, I'd like your attention."

The ten or so people in the room looked toward
the tall man. Reed escorted Mallory to an unoccupied
chair and she sat while he lounged beside her on the
arm. "I'll introduce you to the family later," he said.

Mallory was aware of Reed's jeans-clad thigh very
close to her arm, the bulk of him by her shoulder.
She couldn't seem to control her pulse rate when he
was this close. But when Ryan Fortune began speaking, she focused all her attention on him.

Ryan started. "I would rather this were a happy
occasion, a celebration for Reed and Mallory's marriage."

Everyone looked at them, smiled, and Mallory
blushed. She felt like an imposter.

The patriarch of the Fortune family continued.
"But it's not, and I'll get straight to the reason I
asked you here. Clint Lockhart has escaped from
prison."

Four

Stunned silence met Ryan Fortune's announcement. He frowned and continued. "While Clint was being transferred to another prison yesterday, the prison van was involved in an accident. He managed to escape. The guard shot at him, but the authorities don't know if he was hit. The guard had been injured in the accident and couldn't chase him farther into the woods."

Mallory tried to remember what she had read about Clint Lockhart when the murder of Sophia Barnes Fortune had been front-page news and Lily had been blamed for the crime. Ryan's first wife, Janine Lockhart, had been Clint's sister, and Clint had lived on the ranch as one of the cowhands. Janine died of breast cancer, and Ryan had later married Sophia. But after Sophia's murder, scandal sheets had reported her intimate involvement with Clint while she was still married to Ryan. Supposedly, Clint had murdered her because she'd reneged on a promise to cut him in on her divorce settlement from Ryan. Then he'd framed Lily for the murder. Lily's son, Cole Cassidy, had helped link Clint to the crime, and after Clint Lockhart had confessed, he'd been given a life sentence.

But now....

The troubled expression on Ryan's face warned

them before his words did. "We all know how badly
Clint hates this family, and I wouldn't put it past him
to try to do more harm. I'm hiring extra security,
especially around Mary Ellen and Sam's house. Since
she's his sister, the authorities believe he may try to
contact her. I called Sam, and they're going to cut
their vacation short and return tomorrow. Authorities
really don't think Clint will get this far before he's
caught, but I'd like you all to stick close to home. I
don't want the Double Crown to feel like a prison to
you, though, and I just ask that you not go anywhere
alone, not until he's apprehended. Are we agreed on
that?"

Everyone nodded.

Ryan draped his arm around his wife's shoulders.
"On the other hand, Clint Lockhart has taken up too
much of our time and attention over the past year.
Rosita has fixed a spread for anyone who's hungry,
so go and enjoy it so she knows she did a good job."
Then he forced a smile and motioned toward the dining room.

Reed leaned close to Mallory. "Just to fill you in
on some background…as Ryan said, Mary Ellen is
Clint's sister. She married Ryan's brother, Cameron,
who's now deceased. Her new husband, Sam, is a
security expert. Mary Ellen and Cameron built that
house we passed earlier. After Cameron died, she
stayed close to the family and eloped with Sam about
six months ago."

"This family's endless," Mallory murmured.

"Just about," Reed quipped. "I haven't even met
all my cousins yet. C'mon, let me introduce you to
some people. They'll want to meet my new wife."

Mallory didn't enjoy playing a role. Reminding

herself that Reed had been engaged to someone else a few days ago, she told herself that she really didn't belong here, didn't really belong with Reed. But she let him guide her toward a group of family members.

He introduced her to Dallas Fortune, the son Ryan had been talking to earlier, and his wife Maggie; another son, Matthew, and his wife Claudia; Cruz and his wife Savannah. Rosita introduced Mallory to her husband Ruben and explained that Maggie was her daughter.

Finally Zane came over to them, a pretty brunette on his arm. She wore her hair pulled back in a ponytail and her large blue gray eyes twinkled. "My wife Gwen," Zane said with a crooked smile. "The woman who tamed me."

Gwen lightly jabbed him in the ribs. "Your nose is going to grow," she teased with a loving smile. "I didn't tame him, I redirected his energy."

Zane rolled his eyes and shook his head.

As Ryan joined them, he cast a concerned look at Mallory. "The rest of us are used to dealing with Clint and the trouble he's brought down upon us. I hope I didn't scare you. I just want everyone to be careful."

Reed put his arm around her and pulled her against his shoulder. Again she tensed for a moment, then made herself relax. Right now, being this close to Reed seemed more dangerous than any harm an escaped convict could do.

"I'll make sure she's kept safe," Reed told his uncle.

"You know, I've been thinking since you got off the plane this afternoon, we ought to give you a real wedding, with a cake and all the trimmings,'' Ryan suggested.

"No," they both said quickly.

Gwen and Zane exchanged looks, and Ryan asked, "Why ever not?"

"We really appreciate the thought," Reed responded for both of them, "but we don't want any fuss."

"Right," Mallory agreed.

"I guess this *is* a honeymoon of sorts for you before you go back to Australia," Ryan concluded. "I imagine Reed's told you that two of his brothers and his sister are coming over in a few weeks," he remarked.

"I, uh, we haven't talked about a whole lot yet," Mallory said, feeling guilty because everyone was being so nice.

Zane chuckled. "Newlyweds aren't supposed to do a lot of talking. And speaking of being newlyweds, I think Gwen and I will turn in. Our kids will be up at the crack of dawn."

Gwen told Mallory, "He became an instant dad of three when he married me six months ago."

Zane clasped his wife's hand and gave her a little tug toward him. "See you later," he said, then added, "or maybe not. How about the four of us go out sometime? We can show Mallory some of San Antonio before Dawson gets back."

Reed nodded, and Zane and Gwen left the great room, going down a hall toward a suite of rooms. After speaking to them a few minutes longer, Ryan also moved away to mingle.

Looking down at Mallory, Reed asked, "Would

you like to get something to eat? Or go back to the cabin?''

Pretense wasn't her style. At least back at the cabin, they both knew where they stood. "It's been a long day. If you don't mind, I'd like to go back."

"Everyone will understand if we leave."

Because they were supposed to be on their honeymoon.

After a round of goodbyes and winks and smiles, they left. A full moon lighted their way as they drove back to the cabin. Once there, Mallory climbed out of the truck and took a deep breath of the night air. It was much different here than in San Francisco, starker in some ways, the beauty more primitive. But she liked it.

As they walked up the path to the front door, she made sure her elbow didn't touch Reed's, and as he opened the door and she passed by him, she made sure she didn't breathe in his scent or glance at his rugged profile. There was too much about Reed Fortune that she found as primitive as the Texas landscape.

Reed followed Mallory into the cabin. She had been quiet all evening, and he felt he had to address the reason. Apparently her mind had been on the same track as his because she stopped in the doorway to the bedroom. "How long were you engaged?"

Since he'd met Mallory, Stephanie had definitely gotten pushed to the background, and he was beginning to wonder why. After all, he'd planned a future with the woman and now, only a few days after their breakup, he seemed to be over her. The loyal, committed type, he'd waited a long time to settle down.

He should be more upset, but he didn't know how to explain that to Mallory.

"A year and a half," he answered, hanging his Stetson on the rack by the door.

"Why did she break it off?"

"She married another man."

"I see," Mallory said quietly, and he could sense exactly what she was thinking—that she'd been absolutely right about him marrying her in a fit of pique or using her to salve a bruised ego. He couldn't tell her she was wrong.

"Do you want to take a shower?" she asked, changing the subject. "If you do, I'll go outside and wait."

"Going outside alone at night isn't a good idea."

"Then I can wait in the kitchen," she said.

She was making it clear she didn't want to be anywhere near him. That not only annoyed him but made him angry, as well.

"You can wait in the living room and be comfortable while you're doing it. I'm not going to throw open the door to the bathroom, toss you on the bed, and have my way with you. Didn't I prove that already?"

"Although you explained what happened when we got back to your motel room, I don't have to believe it. Maybe you're the one who passed out first."

Exasperated with the tension between them as well as with his desire for her, he snapped, "Wait where you want, Mallory. Just don't go outside alone, and keep the door locked." His voice was rough and authoritative, and he could see that she didn't like it. It didn't matter. He was going to keep her safe whether she wanted to be safe or not.

Moving away from the bedroom archway, she went into the kitchen, took a glass from the cupboard, and turned on the spigot.

Reed went to the bedroom and snatched a pair of sleeping shorts from the chest of drawers. She was a spoiled, pampered princess and he shouldn't care what she thought. Yet he did.

When he emerged from the bathroom fifteen minutes later, she was sitting at the small table, a sketch pad and pencil in hand.

"What are you doing?" he asked, trying to make conversation.

"Nothing important."

Warning himself to be patient with her, he tried again. "You mentioned you did an apprenticeship. What kind?"

"I have a degree in interior design. I was working with an interior decorator."

"You said your parents didn't like that idea?"

"My mother and my stepfather believed I should hide my degree under a bushel basket, play tennis, and attend charity functions."

"Is that what Bentley wanted you to do, too?"

"I'm not sure what he wanted me to do. It seems I'm not a very good judge of men or their motives."

Her tone, as well as the underlying meaning in her words, made Reed want to shake her or kiss her senseless. To keep himself from doing either, he went to the closet in the bedroom and took out a sheet and a pillow. Then he unfolded the sofa bed.

Standing, Mallory took her sketch pad and went into the bedroom.

He heard her moving around in there, then her footsteps as she went into the bathroom. After he lay on the sofa bed, he turned out the light on the end table. Unfortunately for him, he glanced toward the bedroom when he heard her come out of the bathroom and saw her outlined by the glow of her bedside lamp—every delectable curve was evident under her nightgown.

Swearing under his breath, he turned in the other direction, plumped his pillow, and knew this was going to be a very long night.

When Mallory awakened the following morning after a restless night, all too conscious that Reed had lain practically naked out on the sofa bed, she knew he wasn't in the cabin. Some sixth sense told her when he was close and when he wasn't. Sliding out of bed, she pulled on a robe, belted it, and went out to the kitchen. There was a note on the table.

Mallory—
I'm at Cruz Perez's ranch this morning, working with him. Stay in the cabin with the door locked. I'll be back around noon. If you need anything, Cruz's number is on the refrigerator.
                                              Reed

Though she breathed a sigh of relief at Reed's absence, she missed his presence. It didn't make any sense.

After she brushed her teeth and showered, she dressed and again sat at the table with her sketch pad, doodling, making a diagram of the cabin, filling in blank walls and empty spaces. She jotted down colors that would be the most striking and types of art she would use to decorate. When the door opened and

Reed came in, she was surprised at how the time had flown. As he hung his hat on the rack, she saw his jeans were dusty and his shirt damp with sweat. His gaze swept over her shorts and blouse, the same outfit she'd worn last evening.

"I thought I'd give you a little time to yourself this morning," he said.

"I appreciate that," she returned politely.

He frowned. "Rosita and Ruben have invited us to an early Sunday dinner. Are you interested?"

"Are you?" she asked.

He let out an exasperated sigh. "We wouldn't have to cook, and their house is air-conditioned. Cruz and his wife and Dallas and Maggie will be there, so you won't have to worry about making conversation with me, though we should try to be cordial. Maybe a little more than cordial so they believe we *are* married."

The phone rang. Since she was closer to it, she picked it up, glad for the interruption. But at her "Hello?" she heard an all-too-familiar voice.

"Mallory," Winston said. "Are you feeling better?"

Remembering the scene in the motel parking lot in Reno, she gripped the phone tighter. "I was feeling just fine until you tried to kidnap me."

"I know you saw it that way," he said placatingly, "but you have to understand the position I was in. I'm a man of stature in San Francisco, Mallory. How do you think I felt being stood up at the altar and left to explain where you were? Wouldn't any man be angry?"

"You still had no right to try to force me into the car with you."

Silence met her. "I still want to marry you, Mallory. No other woman has ever been as important to me as you are.''

Maybe because she could see Winston more clearly now, she heard the manipulation in his voice. He would do or say anything to get what he wanted and maybe more than that if he had to. She glanced at Reed. "I'm already married, Winston."

''You married Reed Fortune as some sort of rebellion. I can forgive you that, Mallory. I can also give you time if that's what you need. I want you to think about the life we could share here in San Francisco and, when you're ready, I'll be here waiting for you.''

If she'd thought Winston was going to give up, she'd been wrong. "Winston, it's not going to happen."

As if he didn't hear her, he continued. ''I can be a very patient man, Mallory. Give me a call any time, day or night, and I'll come for you.''

''Winston—''

''Think about it, Mallory. Think about us. I'll be in touch.''

Before she could make the point that he shouldn't bother, he hung up.

She didn't want to admit it, but she feared Winston Bentley IV, and if she'd thought she could end this marriage to Reed before Dawson returned, she'd been wrong.

''He's not going to give up, is he?'' Reed asked.

''No.'' She tried to keep her fear out of her voice, but she wasn't sure she'd managed it. ''I guess we'll have to play at being married a little bit longer.''

''It doesn't feel like playing,'' Reed said wryly.

The tension from last night as well as the knowledge of his fiancée still haunted her. "Look, Reed, if there's something you want to say—"

"There's something I'd like to *do*," he returned, stepping closer to her.

The silver glints in his eyes had been there the night they'd met. She remembered his kiss, the feel of his arms around her, and she stood perfectly still so he wouldn't guess how his words excited her.

They stared at each other for a few long moments and then Reed spun away. "I'm going to change, then we can go."

As he went into the bedroom, she sagged against the wall and realized she couldn't go on denying that she wanted to taste his kiss again, no matter why he'd married her.

Sunday afternoon and evening at the Perez house passed pleasantly...yet it was unsettling whenever Mallory's gaze met Reed's...whenever they pretended to be newlyweds as he casually draped his arm across her shoulders or around her waist. For most of the afternoon, the men watched a baseball game while the women sat in the kitchen and talked. Mallory enjoyed herself immensely just listening to the anecdotes of being part of a large family. After a light supper, she mentioned to Rosita that she needed to learn to cook. Rosita insisted she take along one of her favorite cookbooks and told Mallory if she had any questions, she should call her. It had been an enjoyable day.

But later Sunday evening, as Mallory and Reed readied themselves for bed, the tension between them was tauter than the night before.

Reed rose at 5:00 a.m. Monday morning and Mallory pretended to be asleep as he dressed in the bathroom, then left the cabin. Before they'd turned in, he'd told her he'd be working at the Double Crown for the day. She sketched a little, and made tuna salad sandwiches for them for supper. That had been easy enough, and at least she didn't have to worry about burning something on the stove. The silence between them during the meal was awkward, though, and after she cleaned up the dishes, she sat on the patio in the garden and read until darkness chased her inside. She found Reed working on a laptop computer, but he turned in early, as did she. Mallory was well aware that he hadn't fallen asleep right away—she could hear the squeak of the springs in the sofa bed each time he turned.

By Tuesday afternoon, she was going stir crazy and when she saw her car pull up outside, she almost cheered. As a lanky cowboy got out and came up the walk, she opened the screen door and gave him a big smile.

"Hello, ma'am. Over at the Double Crown, they told me you'd be waiting for these." He dangled the keys in his fingers and handed them to her.

"Thank you so much, Mr.—"

"Conroy. Matt Conroy. Reed said you were in my place when you were in Reno."

"The Golden Spur."

"Right."

"I didn't expect you until tonight or tomorrow."

He shrugged. "I have a friend in New Mexico. I stopped there a few hours to sleep, then trucked on down."

"I'm just so glad you could drive the car here like this. I've been lost without it."

"When Reed said he'd pay my expenses down and airfare back, I couldn't refuse. It's given me a chance to spend a few days with my family and friends."

She didn't like the idea that Reed had taken care of all the expenses. "Are you sure I don't owe you anything?"

"Not a thing, ma'am. But I wouldn't mind using your phone to call my brother. He's going to pick me up."

"Where do you need to go?" she asked.

"Just about five miles down the main road."

"If you show me how to get there, I'll be glad to take you," she said, eager to get out.

"You don't have to do that."

"I want to. I'd like to look around a little. I haven't been away from here since I got here. Just let me get my purse and we can go."

Mallory had been blessed with a good sense of direction. After she dropped Matt off at his brother's house, she used the map of San Antonio she had stored in her glove compartment in preparation for her visit with Dawson to explore. She almost took the road to Leather Bucket. The town with the unique name teased her curiosity. But instead she took the highway that led to San Antonio and couldn't help but turn into a mall. She had the urge to brighten up the cabin since she was spending so much time there, and knew it wouldn't take much. She really shouldn't spend any of her nest egg, yet she somehow felt she needed to prove to Reed that she was as capable in interior design as he was in training horses. Within an hour and a half, she'd filled the back seat of her sports car with bags and parcels, tied the trunk down over a very small secretary she could take to an apartment or an office, and headed back to the Double Crown.

Pulling into the gravel drive beside the cabin, she saw Reed's truck already parked there. Surprised that he was back before she was, she grabbed two of the bags from the back seat and hurried inside.

But he met her not far from the door, his expression thunderous. "Where in the blue blazes have you been?"

She didn't like his tone or his authoritative stance. "Not that I have to answer to you for every minute of my time, but I took Matt to his brother's and then went shopping."

"Don't you have an ounce of sense in that head of yours? Didn't you hear a word Ryan said Saturday night? He specifically warned you about going anywhere alone."

She'd completely forgotten about the warning or the threat. Excited about having her car again, thrilled to explore an area where she'd be living, anxious to just get away for a while and get some perspective on everything, she'd forgotten about Clint Lockhart. But Reed's attitude made her feel defensive, not apologetic. "I wasn't alone. I left with Matt Conroy, and Clint Lockhart wouldn't know me from one of the prison guards."

"Clint Lockhart makes it his business to know everything about the Fortunes, whether he's in jail or out of it, and I'll bet the same goes for Winston Bentley. I want your promise that you won't go driving around alone again."

Annoyed because he could possibly be right, but hating the feeling that he was treating her like a teenager who didn't know what was good for her, she started for the bedroom with the packages. "I'm not promising you anything."

He caught her arm, his grip hard. "I'll put a bodyguard on you if I have to."

She tried to wrench away, but he wouldn't release her. "You wouldn't dare."

"Try me." His blue eyes were icy, his jaw set.

"Let me go."

"Do you really want me to let you go, Mallory?"

She could see the desire in his eyes and knew it was probably mirrored in hers. All she had to do was to stop pulling away, and he'd kiss her. All she had to do was to lean closer to him. But then she thought of his fiancée and of something her own mother had confided in her once. She'd be a fool if she let Reed Fortune kiss her again.

This time when she wrenched away, he released her, but he still looked angry.

"Think about what I said, Mallory. If you don't want someone watching you twenty-four hours a day, we'd better come to an understanding."

Then he left the cabin, letting the screen door bang behind him. A few minutes later she heard the truck start up and he backed off the gravel, his wheels spinning. She didn't know where he was headed or when he'd be back, but she knew he *would* be back because he was that kind of man.

Shaken by the passion as much as the anger she'd felt emanating from Reed, she brought in the rest of the packages from her car, as well as the small desk, determined to do something constructive instead of worrying about what Reed thought of her or when he'd be back.

She'd spent very little really in the broader scheme

of things. The desk fit perfectly to the right of the door, with a straw weaving she'd found on a bargain table hanging above it. The Native American throw rugs she'd bought at a stand in the mall's parking lot added the first bright splashes of color in front of the sofa, under the table, and beside the bed. Two different size ceramic pots in the same shade of green as the sofa and the bolder colors of the rugs she positioned to one side of the rough-hewn mantel. She balanced them with a white pillar candle atop a black wrought-iron stand on the other side. The cabin started looking more like a home when she threw an inexpensive throw patterned with horses over the back of the sofa and laid two multicolored handwoven place mats on the table. Then she set a terra-cotta pot with dried flowers in the center of the table and plumped two throw pillows in natural shades from tan to deep brown, arranging one on either end of the sofa. She'd wanted to look for curtains but hadn't taken measurements before she'd left.

She hadn't thought before she'd left.

With a sigh she set a ceramic replica of a mare and her foal on the coffee table. She'd done a lot with a little and was pleased. If Reed didn't like it, she'd take it all with her.

It was dark when Reed returned, and she'd turned on all the lamps so he could see the changes she'd made. But when he unlocked the door and came inside, he took one look around and didn't comment on any of them.

So that's the way he was going to be. Fine. It didn't matter to her.

She sat at the table reading a magazine about the attractions in San Antonio while he showered. But when he came into the living room in black cotton sleeping shorts and unfolded the sofa, she sneaked a peek at him. His hair was still damp from his shower and lay against the nape of his neck. His tawny chest hair whorled down the middle of his chest and slipped under the band of his shorts. His shoulders and arms were muscled, and his stomach flat. She saw a mark on his back, just above his waist. Was it the Fortune birthmark? But he turned out the lamps, and she took the hint, going into the bathroom to change into her nightgown. Then she sat on the side of the bed and switched off the light.

As she did, she knew she had to tell him something. "Reed?"

There was a pause. "Yes."

"I'll be more careful. I won't leave the Double Crown by myself, and I'll let you know where I go."

Just as she thought he wasn't going to answer, he did. "Then I guess I won't have to hire a twenty-four-hour bodyguard for you."

He wasn't giving an inch. She settled herself into bed, thinking she'd given hers.

An hour later, still awake, she slipped out of bed and softly padded to the kitchen. After she turned on the small light over the counter, she opened the refrigerator door, trying not to make any noise.

But as she reached for the milk carton, Reed's deep voice carried to her. "I would have brought the desk in for you if you'd asked." Then he added, "The cabin looks homier, Mallory. You did a good job."

Five

Standing in the archway to the bedroom, Reed watched Mallory. She was as beautiful in sleep as she was the rest of the day. After she'd come out to the kitchen last night, he'd heard her get back into bed and then sensed she had fallen asleep—unlike the past two nights.

He shouldn't have lost his temper with her yesterday, but when he'd come back and found the cabin empty, fear had gripped him so vigorously he couldn't shake it loose. She was used to the best money had to offer and the freedom to go with it. She'd lost that freedom for the time being and he sensed her restlessness with it. Or maybe it was just restlessness with him, being married to someone and not really being married.

The urge to slide into the bed beside her, brush her hair from her cheek and kiss her with some of the pent-up desire he felt was so strong that he turned away from her, folded the sofa into place and went into the bathroom.

As he dressed, he tried to ignore his thoughts about the woman sleeping in the bed outside the door. When he'd come home last night and found the cabin more like a home than a stopover point, it had unsettled him. The cabin now looked like a place where two people could start a life! Yet he'd known decorating it had simply been a project to Mallory, to give herself something to do.

Buckling his belt, he decided to grab something at the bunkhouse for breakfast instead of disturbing Mallory by making noise in the kitchen. But when he put his hand on the doorknob to leave the cabin, a soft, sleepy voice called out to him.

"Reed?"

He steeled himself against the lure of it. "I'm leaving, Mallory."

"Where will you be today?"

"Over at the Double Crown's training arena."

"I'll make supper," she called.

He had to smile. "You're sure?"

"I want to try one of the recipes Rosita gave me."

"See you later, then."

"Later," she murmured as he opened the door and left. She'd probably go back to sleep until noon. He'd alert the security guards that she was home alone and ask them to be particularly watchful.

Midmorning he realized he'd been wrong about Mallory sleeping until noon when he saw her snazzy car pull up to the gravel area beside one of the corrals. She was dressed in a pair of black slacks, a white cotton blouse and natural leather shoes that tied. When she saw him, she quickly walked toward him. The swing of her hair, the ruffle of her bangs in the breeze and the graceful movement of her body made him take a deep breath.

"Is something wrong?" he asked when she reached the corral.

She smiled at him. "No, I came to work."

His gaze took another sweep of her. "Work?"

"I know I have to get a pair of jeans and some

boots, but for now this will have to do. I can't sit in the cabin and do nothing all day, Reed. Isn't there something I can do here? I love horses...."

She might love horses in theory, but working with them was another matter entirely and required know-how. "You'll get dirty," he said succinctly.

"That doesn't matter. I can wash this, and the shoes... Well, they'll just be my work shoes."

To hide another smile, he swiped off his Stetson and ran a hand through his hair. If she wanted work to do, he'd give her work. After today, maybe she'd go up to the house and help Rosita instead of distracting him!

"Follow me," he ordered, setting his hat back on his head.

He led her into one of the barns, aware of her light footsteps behind him. The wranglers were exercising the mares from this barn and it was still, except for the flies and dust motes dancing in the sunlight.

Opening one of the stall doors, he nodded to the hay and the smell emanating from it. "The stalls need to be mucked out. The pitchfork is over there." He pointed to a partition. "As well as anything else you might need—a shovel or broom. Just push the mess into a pile outside. Any questions?"

The crestfallen look on her face was priceless. She'd probably make up an excuse and find something else to do fairly quickly. Staring at him for a few moments, she didn't look away. Then without a word she went toward the partition and grabbed the pitchfork. "You can go back to what you were doing," she said. "I'll be fine in here."

He'd give her fifteen minutes tops, then expect to see her headed toward her car.

A half hour later he went to the barn to check on her. Her nose wrinkled as she shoveled hay and horse droppings into a pile on the outside walkway to the barn. She must have found a rubber band somewhere and tied her hair up in a ponytail. She'd also rolled up her blouse sleeves. Smudges of dirt already marred the pristine material. He thought about teasing her, then decided that would be pushing his luck after their go-around yesterday. Still betting she'd leave before lunch, he went back to the corral and the colts, which he understood much better than Mallory.

Time got lost as he eased the young horses into halters, handled them and spoke to them gently. It was the basis of all the training he did. But when Hank, a grizzled old cowhand, called to him to ask him if he was having lunch at the bunkhouse, he remembered Mallory. After returning a colt to the pasture, he saw that her car was still there. Surprised, he went to the barn and found her inside, mucking out yet another stall.

"Lunch break," he announced, admiring her grit in sticking to the job this long.

"I have one more stall to clean out. I think I'll do that, then get lunch back at the cabin. I'll have to get supper started."

"What are we having?" he asked.

She tilted her head and gave him a smug smile. "It's a surprise."

He pretty much knew what was in the freezer. "Mallory, you don't have to go to a lot of trouble. I could just cook steaks on the grill."

"I'm stopping at the big house to talk to Rosita and get what I need. I want to make supper, Reed. You've done so much for me already."

He didn't expect gratitude from her, and he had to admit it wasn't particularly what he wanted, either. "All right, then. I'll see you later." As he turned to leave the barn, she called his name.

When he stopped to face her, she said, "I'm sorry about yesterday. I didn't mean to do anything foolish. I didn't even think about Clint Lockhart and Winston. I just wanted to do something useful."

This woman surprised him at every turn, and he wasn't sure he liked the unsettled feeling that it gave him. It was bad enough desire tangled up his thoughts. "Forget about it, Mallory. It's over."

This time when he turned to leave, she didn't stop him. Once outside in the sunshine, he shrugged off the feeling that it *wasn't* over. Mallory wasn't the passive type, and he had a feeling that given a good reason, she'd do the same thing all over again.

It was almost six o'clock when Reed returned to the cabin after going over training schedules with Cruz and Hank for the next month. When his sister Matilda arrived, she could give them a hand, and Cruz could spend more time at his own place. Though Matilda was young, twenty-one, she was almost as good with horses as Reed was, though he'd never admitted that to her. She'd been born a tomboy and insisted that any girl who had five brothers had to be one to survive. The truth was, they were all protective of her and she hated it.

He had to admit he missed her. He missed all of them, in a different way than when he'd gone away to college. Though he'd enjoyed every minute of it, the University of Adelaide had seemed a world away from his home. Now he really *was* a world away.

He should call and tell his folks about Stephanie

before they heard it from mutual friends. And then there was Mallory...

Thoughts of home quickly vanished. The hearty aroma of meat and spices wound around him as he stepped inside the adobe. Even though its thick walls kept it comfortable most of the time, the heat from the oven had infiltrated everywhere and even the ceiling fan wasn't doing much good. Mallory had changed into a tank top and shorts, but her cheeks were flushed and her bangs damp from the time she'd spent in the kitchen. Her hair was still caught up in a ponytail.

"It smells terrific," he said.

"I hope it tastes as good." She sounded worried. But then she went on, "I set the table outside. The oven made it really hot in here."

"Give me ten minutes for a quick shower and I'll be right out."

When he joined her outside, he couldn't believe his eyes, let alone his nose. If the roast beef tasted as good as it looked, he was in for a treat. The broccoli and carrots had been steamed to a perfect color and the bowl of mashed potatoes made his mouth water. "You learned how to do this in one easy lesson?" he asked, amazed.

She winked at him. "I'm a fast learner."

He laughed. "Are you sure Rosita didn't come down here and cook this?" But as soon as the words were out of his mouth, he knew Mallory might take the remark as an insult. "I'm teasing," he added gently.

She gave him an impish smile. "I know you are." Then she held up her right hand. "I swear I did this on my own, and I only called Rosita twice." They both laughed together this time as they sat at the table and started in on their plates. When Reed took the first bite, he noticed Mallory watching him. Swallowing, he remarked, "It's good, Mallory."

"Really?" she asked, looking concerned.

"Really."

Her hazel eyes sparkled with his compliment and he wanted to lean across and kiss her, yet he didn't want to disrupt the welcome camaraderie that had sprung up. Although the sexual tension that had vibrated between them from the moment they'd met hadn't lessened, they ate in an almost companionable silence.

When they'd finished, Mallory stood and picked up both of their plates. "I almost hate to go back inside."

He stood, too, and suddenly had an idea he hoped would please her. "Then let's not go back in."

"I have to do the dishes."

"We'll let them soak in the sink. I want to take you somewhere."

"Where?"

"You'll see," he said mysteriously. "But you might want to grab your bathing suit and if you don't have one, you could try skinny-dipping."

Her eyes widened and she assured him, "I have one."

Chuckling, he took his plate from her and followed her around the side of the adobe. A few minutes later they were sitting in the truck, bumping over a gravel access road. Soon, even the gravel disappeared and they traveled on the packed earth. Slowing as stands of cedar grew thicker, he finally stopped beside a live oak. "We're here. We don't have to walk far."

He came around to Mallory's side of the truck and opened the door for her. When he offered her his hand, her gaze met his. The electricity between them practically buzzed, but she took his hand and used it for leverage as she stepped down to the ground. They walked side by side through the range grass until they broke through a line of oaks.

When she stopped, so did he. "How lovely," she murmured as if entering a holy place.

He felt that way about this spot. The descending sun was a fiery red ball reflected in the calm, cool water of the lake where a willow dropped its branches. Tall grass grew along the north and west borders. Sparkles of sunlight danced to the south and east as the bare earth embraced the water.

"It's spring fed," Reed explained, "so it's cold."

"Right now I could use a little cold," she said with a smile.

He handed her one of the towels he'd brought, laid his on the ground and pulled off his boots and socks. When his hands went to the snap on his jeans, Mallory asked, "What are you doing?"

"I'm going swimming."

Unfastening his fly, he let his jeans drop to the ground.

Mallory backed up, but her eyes dropped below his waist. He was wearing black briefs, not a bathing suit.

"I didn't bring a suit with me." He shrugged.

She quickly spun around and peered at the lake.

"Mallory." He kept his voice gentle. "You've seen me naked. I've seen you."

"Not when I was fully conscious of what I was

doing,'' she retorted, glancing over her shoulder and keeping her eyes steadily on his.

Instead of being a bond, the night they'd spent together in that motel room was a barricade. ''I'm going in,'' he said gruffly.

Mallory watched as Reed strode into the water and dove under and swam out to the middle. Her hands were trembling and she realized her attachment to this man scared her. All he had to do was smile at her, let alone bare his chest or more, and her insides quivered with a longing she didn't recognize. She'd been brought up to be a proper lady, and she didn't understand what had happened that night in Reno...why simple rebellion had turned into marriage to a man she didn't know.

The temperature hadn't eased much and standing here watching Reed wasn't going to help her cool off. Choosing a compact clump of cedars for a changing screen, she slipped behind them and quickly removed her clothes. The little devil who'd prompted her to sit at Reed's table at the Golden Spur made her wonder, *What if he saw you like this, and you were fully conscious?*

The excited tingles that danced through her body made her grab her pink bikini bottom and slip it on quickly. When she fastened the top, she suddenly realized that this bathing suit wasn't a whole lot better than being naked around Reed. But it would have to do. Leaving her clothes, she snatched her towel and carried it to the spot where Reed had waded in.

She stepped into the water slowly. It was cold but felt delicious against her hot skin. Gradually she went in farther, then splashed water on her neck and arms. Finally she ducked under the water and swam across the lake. They both swam for a while until Mallory floated into more shallow water and stood, appreciating the beautiful sunset, the orange, purple and pink streaks shooting through what was left of the blue sky. She heard a splash of water and sensed Reed swimming up beside her. When he stood, she could feel the immense masculine power of him, as awe inspiring in some ways as the sunset.

Clasping her shoulder, he nudged her around to face him. His hair was wet and he must have brushed it from his forehead when he came out of the water. Droplets glittered on his shoulders and in his chest hair under the last rays of the sun. "Are you glad you came?" he asked.

She nodded, her voice sticking in her throat. She couldn't take her eyes from his, and caution warned her to move away. But she couldn't. Not when anticipatory excitement was making her heart race and her breaths shallow.

"I shouldn't have lost my temper with you yesterday," he admitted.

It seemed hard for him to make the apology, and she guessed that it didn't come easy for him.

"Does that happen often?" she teased lightly, so he'd know she'd accepted it.

But he didn't smile. "Only when I care about something a great deal."

The power in his blue gaze seemed to pull her closer, and she recognized it as desire. She felt her body leaning slightly toward his. His hand on her shoulder slipped to the small of her back, and she knew she could still pull away. She should be cautious. She should run....

His head bent to hers and she raised her mouth for his kiss.

His hand was large and gentle on her back, and soon it was joined by his other one in a sense-stirring duet caressing her spine. When he reached her buttocks, he raised her to him and his tongue invaded her mouth. She gasped at the erotic contact and wrapped her legs around him. He was hot and hard, and she'd never known a sensation so pleasurable, so fulfilling, yet not quite fulfilling enough. His briefs, her suit, both wet, were little less than a film between them, making the contact even more tantalizing. His groan echoed through her and she responded to his tongue by stroking against it, wrapping her arms around his neck and holding on for dear life.

Reed finally broke the kiss and when her gaze found his, she saw controlled desire there. "I want my hands over every part of you," he said. "I want to sink into you until the sun comes up. Is that what you want?"

Still dazed by a passion she didn't understand and a desire that was as new as her marriage, she could hardly comprehend what he was saying. She knew he was talking about pleasure and satisfaction and sex. Isn't that what had gotten them into this mess? Because his fiancée had dumped him? How could she have forgotten that even for a moment?

"No," she said breathlessly, and then louder, "No!"

His expression changed. The desire faded from his eyes and became a blue wall. "Once is enough, Mallory. There's nothing wrong with my hearing."

She remembered Winston trying to kidnap her and how many times she'd said no. Her wishes hadn't mattered to him and she wondered if it would have been any different in the bedroom. But Reed—

Suddenly she remembered too well what her mother had confided in her when she was a teenager. She'd come into her mother's room and found her sitting at her vanity, a stack of letters in her hand.

"What are they?" Mallory had asked.

Her mother had said, "I was cleaning out the closet and found them with your father's things. They're letters from his first wife, Dawson's mother." And then she told Mallory something Mallory had never forgotten. "He wouldn't have kept them unless they meant something to him, Mallory. I've always suspected he came to me because of a midlife crisis and once the damage was done to his marriage, he couldn't go back. There's a lesson here, honey. They had that 'always' kind of love, and that kind lasts forever. Your father is my true love, but I'm not his. If I hadn't been blinded by my love for him, I would have realized it before we married. Don't ever marry a man who still has ties to another woman."

Reed still had ties to another woman.

His voice was a husky rasp when he said, "Just drop your legs and I'll put you down."

She'd wrapped her legs around him to fit to him…to give them both a taste of fulfillment. But a taste wasn't nearly enough, and she wasn't about to give any more when he still had feelings for his fiancée. She suspected Reed wasn't the type of man who could love a woman one minute and forget about her the next.

Even though she unwound her legs, she felt his

arousal as he lowered her. Still, embarrassment didn't keep her from asking, "Reed?"

His hands slipped from her and he stepped back. "What?" His voice was gritty with a desire she could still feel, too.

"Were you involved with anyone before Stephanie?"

"Involved? You mean, in a serious relationship?"

"Yes."

"No. Stephanie was the first."

Her heart sinking, Mallory turned away from him and made her way to the bank.

"Mallory, it's over with Stephanie," he called to her.

She stopped for a moment. "Only because she married someone else."

Silently he watched her step onto the bank and head for the clump of cedars. She could feel his eyes on her but she didn't turn around and she didn't slow her steps. The sooner she dressed, the sooner she'd forget how Reed's hands had felt on her skin and how his body had felt pressed against hers.

The Texas night was unusually quiet as sweat dripped from Clint Lockhart's brow and down his back. A lone coyote barked in the distance, startling him. They couldn't have the dogs after him yet here. They didn't know where he was. Why hadn't the guard who'd shot him come after him?

He didn't know. He didn't care.

His bad luck had changed to good when the prison van tried to pass a slow-moving pickup in front of them. Doing at least sixty-five in the passing lane, a sports car had come at them out of nowhere. The van had swerved to avoid a head-on collision, slid into a ditch, and rolled over. In spite of his chains and cuffs, Clint and two other convicts who weren't badly injured managed to get out. Both guards had been unconscious, and they'd gotten the keys and had their restraints off in a matter of minutes. One guard must have come around as Clint had gone through the woods instead of turning north like the other two prisoners. He'd only managed about twenty yards when he'd heard a shout, then a warning gunshot fired into the sky. But he'd kept on running.

Moments later he'd heard a second shot and felt the burning pain in his leg, knowing he'd been hit. Still he'd kept running.

When he'd reached the clearing and the railroad tracks, he'd heard the sound of a train. Then he'd watched and he'd waited. All that ranch work and weight lifting at the prison had paid off. His upper body had done what his lower couldn't. After he'd hopped the boxcar, he'd known he was safe…for the time being.

He'd reached San Antonio this morning, but he'd known he couldn't stay around. Not with his face probably on every TV and in all the newspapers. Though his leg throbbed and he felt as if he was burning up, he'd known he had to get out of that area. Managing to grab jeans and a shirt from a washline, he'd thrown his clothes into the river and headed for Leather Bucket. He could lay low there until he decided what he was going to do and how he was going to make the Fortunes pay.

If he could just get rid of this damn dizziness.

He cursed the Fortunes as he had all his life. The last few miles had been tough as he'd dragged his leg, and he knew he needed help but didn't know where to get it. Now, as he hobbled through brush, he thought he saw a light up ahead. His ears were buzzing and he knew he had to be careful, but he headed toward the yellow beam. As he got closer, he realized he'd come upon a ramshackle trailer.

But before he could even think about what to do next, his dizziness became a swirl of blackness, blacker than a starless night. He fought it. He fought the noise in his ears.

But both overpowered him until he felt himself falling, falling....

Six

Mallory lay curled on her side, facing away from the living room archway, when Reed got up the next morning, dressed, and left the cabin. She told herself she shouldn't worry that he was frustrated with her, maybe even angry. She couldn't have sex with him, not when she barely knew him, not in the situation they were in, not with him still thinking about his fiancée. When Mallory made love to a man, she wanted to be the only woman on his mind and be committed to him forever. It wouldn't be a fling or something that just rose out of heat that had no real basis except hormones.

She needed something to keep her busy today, and it wasn't cleaning out stalls. Because she'd ridden most of her life, she knew her way around horses and she wanted to help with them. If Reed showed her what to do, he could leave her alone while she did it. She had to convince him she knew how to ride and could handle herself around the animals. But first she should get Ryan's permission to saddle up.

In the kitchen, she saw the dishes still sitting in the sink from the night before. After they'd come back from the lake in silence, she'd showered and stayed in the bedroom to keep out of Reed's way. She'd heard him in the living room reading a news-paper, heard the pages rustling, and wished she could keep her mind on a magazine article as easily. Finally she'd given up and called it a night, though still aware of every movement Reed had made in the living room, of him entering and leaving the bathroom, of him settling on the sofa bed. They hadn't even said good-night.

After she did the dishes, she dressed and drove to Ryan's house, hoping it wasn't too early. With a smile, Rosita invited her inside and led her to the inner courtyard where Lily and Ryan were having breakfast. It was a beautiful setting. A fountain caught Mallory's eye first, then a vine-covered arbor with an old-fashioned swing under it. The scents of roses and jasmine permeated the morning air. A few glass-topped tables were positioned near the steps leading up to the great room. The one where Lily and Ryan sat offered sweet rolls, corn muffins and a coffee service.

Ryan stood when he saw her and offered her a chair. "Good morning, Mallory. What brings you here so early?"

Before she could answer, Lily asked, "Will you join us for breakfast?"

"I don't want to intrude," Mallory answered them both.

Lily shook her head. "You won't be intruding. We like company." She gave her husband a loving smile.

Ryan pulled out a chair while Lily poured another cup of coffee and motioned to the platter of sweet rolls in the center of the table.

These were such nice people that Mallory wished she could really tell them why she was staying here with Reed. But they had their own concerns with

Clint Lockhart on the loose. "I came to ask your permission to take one of the horses riding."

Picking up his coffee cup, Ryan said, "Reed knows he can use any of the horses anytime he wants."

Mallory wanted to explain tactfully. "Actually, the truth is, I want to show Reed that I know how to handle a horse and can maybe help him while I'm…while we're here."

Lily tilted her head and asked knowingly, "Doesn't he think you're up to the task?"

"I think he thinks I'm more ornamental than functional."

Ryan laughed and Lily gave him a scolding look, but he just patted his wife's hand. "Fortune men tend to be protective of their women. Can you ride?"

"I've been riding since I was five. I also competed in horse shows and spent lots of time around the stable."

"And Reed doesn't know this yet?" Lily asked.

"We're still learning things about each other," Mallory said honestly.

"That can take a lifetime," Ryan suggested, exchanging a look with Lily. "So you want to show Reed what you can do rather just tell him about it."

"Exactly."

Pushing his chair back, Ryan stood. "I'm going to make a call. I'll be right back."

Left alone with Lily, Mallory pulled her coffee cup toward her.

"Reed told Ryan you have a degree in interior design."

"Yes, I do. I just earned my certification in the spring."

"Would you consider helping me redo one of the guest suites?"

"I would love to, but... I'm sure you could hire anyone you want. Are you sure you want *me* to help?"

Lily shook her head. "I don't want to hire an interior decorator who will do the rooms to his or her own taste. I know local craftsmen and potters and weavers and even woodcrafters. But I would like some fresh ideas. If you have time, I could show you the rooms and maybe we could get together again next week for you to share your ideas. If I like them, I'll give you a commission."

This is exactly what Mallory wanted and if Lily liked what she suggested, she could put the commission away toward starting her own shop. She wanted to take as little from Dawson as necessary. "I'll be glad to give you some ideas."

Ryan came through the glass doors from the great room with a smile on his face. "I called Hank down at the barn. He'll introduce you to our best riding horses. You pick out any one you want. He'll also help you saddle up or let you do it yourself, and then he'll tell you exactly where Reed's working," Ryan finished with a wink.

"You don't know how much I appreciate this," Mallory said with a thankful smile.

Reed's uncle grinned at her. "Let's just say I understand the battle of the sexes." He paused, then added, "Most of the time." After he stooped to give his wife a light kiss, he went to the door to the great room. "I'll be in my office if anyone wants me."

Mallory decided she really liked the Fortune family and wished they were truly her own.

After a leisurely cup of coffee and discussion of the barbecue Ryan and Lily had planned for Sunday, Mallory examined the rooms Lily wanted to redecorate. Her mind buzzed with ideas immediately. She questioned Lily about what she liked and didn't like in styles of decorating, how casual she wanted the rooms to be, and whether or not she wanted to embrace light or shut it out. But what Mallory really wanted to do was to go shopping in San Antonio and take a look at native crafts and what the furniture stores offered. But she knew Reed wouldn't let her go alone. Perhaps after today, he'd see her in a different light and realize she had the wits to take care of herself.

An hour later, armed with confidence as well as the jeans and boots Lily had insisted she borrow for riding, Mallory drove to the barn. The jeans were a little big and the boots a little long, but Mallory didn't care. She was going to prove to Reed that she could help him. As she shut the door of her car, Reed wasn't anywhere in sight and she was glad. When she went into the main barn, she saw Hank coming out of the tack room.

He gave her a broad smile. "Ryan tells me you're ready to get saddled up. C'mon over here and I'll show you what you've got to choose from."

Following the old cowhand to a row of stalls, she easily chose a bay gelding with dark brown eyes.

"Dusty Dawn, here, will take you anywhere you want to go and he knows his way back home real good. You want to saddle him up or should I?" Hank asked.

"I'd like to saddle him myself, if you don't mind."

"Don't mind at all. Let's go find you a saddle that fits."

Though she hadn't saddled a horse in a few years, she remembered exactly how to do it. Hank looked on, and she had to smile, knowing that Ryan had probably told him to keep an eye on her. But he gave her a grin and a nod of approval when she was finished. As she led Dusty Dawn outside, Hank pointed to the training arena and a corral behind it. "Reed's over yonder with Cruz. You gonna ride or walk?"

"Ride," she said with certainty.

"Let me hold him for you, then."

A few moments later it felt great to be back in the saddle again. Mallory leaned forward and patted Dusty Dawn's neck, then took the reins from Hank.

The distance to the back of the arena was as far as a good city block and she clicked the bay into a trot. To her satisfaction, she saw Reed in the corral when she was still a distance away. She knew his tan Stetson as well as the set of his shoulders. Cruz was training a horse on a longe line. At twenty yards away, Reed must have heard her coming because he looked up and caught sight of her. She brought Dusty Dawn to a walk and pulled up at the corral gate.

When Reed came over to her, he was frowning. "What do you think you're doing?"

"I'm going for a ride."

"Does anyone know you're out here?"

"I explained to Ryan that I'm an experienced rider and Hank showed me a few horses I might want to use. I chose this one."

"You're not going out there alone."

"Reed, this is the open range. I'll be fine."

"And you need a hat," he continued as if she hadn't spoken. "The Texas sun can be dangerous."

She had to admit she hadn't thought about that. Already the sun was burning her arms. But she wasn't going to give up on this jaunt now. "I won't be gone long."

"You bet you won't because I'm coming with you."

"Look, Reed, you don't own me—" She stopped when she saw Cruz watching them.

"Don't I damn well know that," Reed muttered. "Wait over there under that pecan tree."

"I could give you a ride back to the barn," she said sweetly.

"You want to share the same saddle?"

She hadn't thought of that, either. But before she could protest, he came out of the corral and swung himself up behind her on Dusty Dawn. Then his arms surrounded her and he took the reins, shouting to Cruz, "I'll be back before lunch."

"Stubborn male," she murmured.

She heard him chuckle as he leaned forward and his hat brushed her hair. "A stubborn male who's looking out for you."

With his chest against her back, his breath on her ear, his male scent intoxicating her, she remembered every vivid detail of last night in the lake. "Were you looking out for me last night?" she asked.

"You were as much a part of that kiss as I was."

He was right. He might have initiated it, but she had responded to it as if...

Turning Dusty Dawn toward the barn, he nudged the horse to a faster pace. When they pulled up, he jumped off. "Spirit's turned out," he said with a nod toward the pasture. "I have to get him." Reed's gaze searched hers for a few moments.

She admitted to herself that she'd rather ride with Reed than go riding alone. "I'll wait."

Fifteen minutes later Reed came to meet her on a black stallion that pulled against his reins as if he wanted to take Reed on the ride of his life.

"He's beautiful," Mallory said.

"His name's Brazen Spirit and we get along real well as long as I keep him moving." Coming up beside her, Reed handed her a hat. It had a wired brim for her to shape it and a leather chin strap. Knowing he was right about the sun, she set the brown hat on her head, bringing the brim over her forehead. Then she gave Dusty Dawn a gentle nudge and they started off. She knew Reed was watching her and that she would have to pass some kind of a test. But she didn't mind. That's what this morning was all about.

He led the way over the limestone soil, along cedars and mesquite. This was so different from a groomed bridle path, but she loved the freedom of it. The sky couldn't have been any bluer or the sun any brighter, and as they rode, she felt truly happy for the first time in a long time. When they crested a hill, they left the fence line and rode toward a stand of oaks. The grass became thicker, and Mallory could see cattle in the distance and hear intermittent brays.

On the dramatic black stallion, Reed was the epitome of a Texas cowboy until he spoke and his accent gave him away. "There's a stream just over the rise," he said.

They'd been riding a good part of an hour, and though Mallory loved the feel of a horse under her again, she knew she would probably be stiff tonight. Reed reined to a stop when they reached some oaks, and she could see the stream just a few feet beyond. Dismounting with the ease of a seasoned horseman, he tethered Spirit, then held Dusty Dawn for her as she dismounted. She walked over to the stream and he came to stand beside her.

"Well, how did I do?" she asked, glancing at him.

"Not too bad…for a princess."

When she looked at him, she could see he was teasing. But the term still rankled, and she started to turn away from him. She wanted to make him forget the life she'd left so he'd see her in her own right out here, but maybe that couldn't happen.

His hand on her shoulder stopped her. "Mallory, you're a fine rider. Why didn't you tell me yesterday that you knew your way around horses?"

"Because yesterday you were testing me and I had something to prove."

"And today?" he asked, his voice deep, his blue eyes alive with the desire that she'd glimpsed last night.

He was full of passion, as much passion as that stallion, and if she just said the word— "Today I *still* had something to prove. I can be useful around here, Reed. I can't sit and twiddle my thumbs until Dawson returns."

"You want to ride a fence line?" he teased.

"What I want is for you to take me seriously."

The silence echoed as his gaze probed hers. "I take you very seriously, Mallory."

If she leaned forward, just a little, he'd probably kiss her. But last night's kiss had shaken her too much for her to invite anything like that again anytime soon. So instead of leaning forward, she took a step back. "Then let me help with the horses. I'm sure there's something I can do."

He sighed. "Let me think about it. I'll talk to Cruz and maybe Hank. We'll see what we can come up with."

She wanted to throw her arms around him and give him a hug, but even that could lead to trouble. Instead she just said, "Thank you."

He smiled. "Don't thank me until you see what we find for you."

After they walked along the stream for a short while, they returned to the horses and mounted up. The ride back was easier, not as tense—as if they'd come to an understanding.

When they arrived at the barn, there was a message for Reed to call Zane. Mallory said, "Go ahead. I'll walk the horses."

Reed hesitated only a moment, then went inside.

Using the phone by the tack room, Reed watched Mallory through the open barn door. Damn, if she didn't look just as good on a horse as on the ground. Riding behind her had brought back all the sensations of last night. That bit of a bathing suit she'd worn in the lake had made him crazy, and he'd had to remind himself he was the one who'd suggested the swim. Then when he'd gotten her close, held her against him, all he could think about was the satisfaction that he knew would be good. When she kissed him back as if she wanted it, too—

He thought about Stephanie and his engagement to her. Stephanie had never aroused him the way Mallory did. All Mallory had to do was smile, walk across a room, brush her hair back, and he wanted her more than he had ever wanted any other woman. It didn't make sense to him. He'd planned a life with Stephanie. He'd felt deeply committed to her. But now, it was as if Mallory was the only woman who mattered.

The sound of Zane's voice jolted Reed back to the present. After listening to his cousin's plans, Reed told Zane he'd get back to him. Then he left the barn, jogged over to Mallory, and took Spirit's reins from her hand. "Zane wants us to go out with him and Gwen tomorrow night."

"Do you want to?" she asked.

If they did, he and Mallory would have to act like newlyweds for the evening. On the other hand, being cooped up in the cabin together wasn't much better. He shrugged. "You could see some of San Antonio if we do. We could go to a restaurant along the Riverwalk. On a Friday night, it will be lively."

"I've been reading about the Riverwalk. I'd love to see it."

So she'd realize what they were getting into, he warned, "We're going to have to pretend we're on our honeymoon."

Her expression changed and she didn't look quite as enthusiastic. But then she said, "It'll be good practice. Lily told me they're having a barbecue on Sunday and it sounds as if they've invited a lot of family."

"I guess it will be our first Texas-style barbecue."

When she smiled up at him, he was glad they were going to have at least this "first" together. "So we're on for tomorrow night?" he asked.

She nodded. "We're on."

When she said it, there was a longing inside him

for more than a Friday night date. Last night, Mallory had asked him tough questions about Stephanie. He was beginning to have lots of questions himself about his engagement, but he was afraid if he looked too closely at it, he might not like the answers. But whether he liked them or not, some answers might find him.

Colorful umbrellas and tables dotted the patio of the bistro along San Antonio's Paseo del Rio—the Riverwalk. Mallory tried to take it all in as she and Reed walked along a portion of the scenic three miles with its limestone bridges, bald Cypress-edged walkways, hotels, cafés, shops and restaurants. Reed was quiet tonight. They'd worked at being friendly the past two days. Last evening he'd taken her for a drive, and they'd had a late dinner along the way. Both yesterday afternoon and today, she'd gentled foals with Hank.

River barges cruised up and down the waterway and Mallory thought a ride on one of them would be a lot of fun. But as she and Reed approached a bistro, she spotted Gwen and Zane waiting for them. Zane motioned to them and after they all exchanged greetings. Reed held Mallory's chair for her and pushed her in as she sat. After working in the corral this afternoon, she'd gone back to the cabin, showered, and changed into a colorful, flowered sundress in turquoise and yellow. Reed was wearing bush shorts and a cream polo shirt, and it was the first she'd seen him in anything other than jeans...or without clothes. Tonight, wearing moccasins without socks and without his Stetson, he looked casually sexy. Anytime she got within a foot of him her hair stood up on her neck and tingles ran through her body.

They'd kept up casual conversation in the truck on the way here as Reed pointed out landmarks, and she told him how much she enjoyed working with the foals. But now as he sat close beside her, his arm brushing hers, his thigh mere inches from her sundress, she wondered if playing newlyweds tonight would disturb him as much as it disturbed her.

Gwen and Zane sat close together, their shoulders comfortably brushing. After the waitress handed the four of them menus, Zane remarked, "The crawfish are great."

"The salmon's delicious, too," Gwen added.

They all ordered seafood, then Gwen smiled at Mallory. "So, how do you like San Antonio?"

"I haven't seen much of it yet, but I love the vibrancy and the mixture of cultures."

"The weather's quite a change from San Francisco, I'd imagine," Zane remarked.

Mallory nodded. "No fog."

They all laughed. As Gwen snuggled closer to her husband, he draped his arm around her. "Zane told me you two met at the Golden Spur in Reno. Was it love at first sight?" she asked.

After a moment of tense silence when neither she nor Reed seemed to know what to say, Reed filled the gap. "The Golden Spur is a busy place. I offered to share my table with Mallory and she accepted."

Zane's eyes narrowed. "And then?"

Mallory felt heat rushing to her cheeks and she cast a quick glance at Reed. "There's really not much to tell."

Zane's gaze held questions. He exchanged a look

with his wife, but before he could probe further, a waitress came to the table with a bottle of wine he had ordered. After he smelled the cork and tasted a few sips, he moved to pour some into Mallory's glass, but she quickly put her hand over it. "No, thanks, none for me. That's how I ended up... married," she trailed off, sorry she'd said the thought aloud.

Zane's brows arched.

As Reed shifted in his seat, she looked over at him. He wore a scowl.

"Oh," Zane joked. "Reed plied you with tequila until you said yes."

"Um, not exactly," Mallory responded.

"Maybe I should have tried tequila instead of champagne," Reed said, his voice rough. "It doesn't have bubbles to go to your head."

Sometimes Mallory got the feeling that her lack of memory about that night really bothered him. Because he'd gotten into this situation and now regretted it? Both Gwen and Zane were examining them closely.

"I don't handle champagne very well," Mallory explained, wishing she could remember everything that had happened, especially their wedding.

"You know..." Zane poured wine for Gwen and then for Reed. "It would probably be a good idea if you two took a few days for a honeymoon. I'm surprised you came back from Reno so soon."

Mallory couldn't tell if he was fishing or just making conversation, but neither she nor Reed responded.

Gwen nudged her husband. "We can go dancing later. Or if you want to do something really romantic, we can take a ride on a river barge after dark. Even Zane and I haven't done that yet.''

Needing to change the direction of the conversation, Mallory said, "Tell me about your children. How old are they?"

As Gwen's attention easily turned to descriptions of her children, Reed's mind remained on Mallory. He wished he'd never ordered that bottle of champagne at the Golden Spur. Yet...

If he hadn't, he wouldn't be married to her, and for some reason that was becoming more and more important each day. It shouldn't be—because they had nowhere to go. She wanted to start a life here in San Antonio. He was going back to Australia. She was a virgin who wanted to have their marriage annulled and a city girl who probably wouldn't like her displacement on a ranch for long. Maybe she liked to ride and spend a little time around horses, but there was a lot more to it than that. Even more to the point—she wasn't the type of woman to follow a man around. If she hadn't been independent and on her own before, she intended to be now.

What rankled most was that she was locked into this marriage of convenience against her will. She hadn't chosen to be married to him. She hadn't chosen to live with him or spend time with him, and he'd better well remember that fact. Just because the curve of her smile made his heart race and the brush of her skin against his aroused him was no reason to get involved. He'd keep her safe until Dawson returned and then any responsibility he felt would be over.

As her arm lightly brushed his elbow when she reached for her glass of water, he stiffened. Her gaze met his briefly. Zane asked her a question about San Francisco and she quickly turned her attention to his cousin. Reed picked up his glass of wine but then set it back down. He didn't want his inhibitions to be blunted in any way, shape, or form. Somehow he had to play the part of being a new groom without being affected by it.

Reaching down by the side of her chair, Gwen picked up a leather carrier. "Do you mind if we take some pictures?"

"She's become a real shutterbug since we got married," Zane remarked with a patient smile.

"I just want to make sure we remember all our special moments."

Her husband squeezed her hand.

Reed knew that, at one time, Zane had been a confirmed bachelor. He'd gone from one woman to the next enjoying himself, not knowing he was missing something. Watching Zane and Gwen together, Reed craved something he'd never had, an unshakable bond that time and circumstances couldn't break or end. But craving it and finding it were two different things. Zane was just damn lucky.

Holding her hand out, Mallory offered, "Let me take a picture of the two of you." After Gwen showed her how to use the camera, she snapped two pictures.

But then Zane took the camera from her. "Okay, now it's your turn. Move closer to Reed."

Without looking at him, Mallory inched her chair closer to his.

"Put your arm around her," Zane teased.

Reed knew if he wasn't careful, Zane was going to guess this was a marriage in name only. Curving his arm around Mallory, Reed whispered in her ear, "Act natural."

Her hair brushed his cheek as she relaxed into his arm but he could still feel the tension in her shoulders, the uneasiness of the two of them being this close.

"Reed, smile!" Gwen insisted.

He was having enough trouble controlling parts of his body other than his face, but he did as Gwen asked. Mallory's sundress lapped against his leg as she shifted. But if she was trying to make more room between them, she wasn't succeeding. Her breast pressed against his chest and he almost groaned. Her sweet smell loosened his inhibitions more than any wine ever could. Unable to resist, his arm surrounding her nudged her nearer.

"If we get any closer I'll be in your lap," Mallory murmured.

"That could be almost as pleasurable as sharing a saddle," he breathed against her cheek. He could feel her rapid breathing and his kept pace with hers.

It seemed to take forever for Zane to snap two photographs, and Reed couldn't help but wonder if his cousin was prolonging the process on purpose.

Conversation over dinner revolved around Ryan's barbecue on Sunday and the possibility that Clint Lockhart could be headed toward San Antonio. But with dessert it shifted to what the couples were going to do next for the evening. Reed knew he'd only be putting himself through torture if they went to a club and he and Mallory danced. Instead he suggested walking along the shops and cafés and soaking in the atmosphere. But he should have known it wouldn't be that easy. With the full moon out and tiny white lights decorating all the trees along the river, Gwen suggested they take a ride on one of the barges. It was the longest forty minutes of his life as he kept Mallory close, pretending to be an attentive groom. Afterward as the women freshened up in public rest rooms, Zane sat beside Reed on a bench overlooking the river.

"Marriage changes a man," Zane said conversationally.

Reed remained silent.

"You know, I paid Gwen to pretend to be my steady girlfriend when Lily's daughter Hannah and my good friend Parker got married. I was tired of my sister and sisters-in-law trying to matchmake. The problem was…the pretending became very real." He glanced at Reed. "Do you have anything you want to tell me?"

"No."

"Did you call your family yet?"

"I will this weekend."

"One more question. Have you forgotten about Stephanie?"

Reed had to admit his thoughts didn't land on her frequently, and as he thought about going home again tonight and sleeping only ten feet away from Mallory, there was definitely only one woman on his mind.

And he didn't know what the hell to do about it.

Seven

A fan hummed. Clint had been hearing that buzzing for a long time and, at first, thought it came with the dizziness. He'd awakened before, and someone had held a glass of water to his lips. One time it had been pitch-black, another— Hell, he hadn't been able to tell reality from nightmare. As he opened his eyes, he raised his hand to a cool cloth on his forehead and saw someone sitting on a chair beside the sofa. He went on guard immediately. Had they caught him? Where had they taken him? If he had to fight his way out....

He felt so damn weak.

Before he could raise himself up, he felt a slight hand on his shoulder. "Stay still," a woman's soft voice said.

The overhead light in the trailer shone on her. As he looked her over, he knew he had nothing to fear from this slight thing. A good Texas wind could blow her into the next county. As he always did with women, he made a thorough examination of her in a few seconds—limp, light brown hair that had seen a peroxide bottle at some time, pure blue eyes that were older than the few lines on her face. She couldn't be much over forty and there wasn't enough weight on her to hardly make any curves.

He was good with women, always had been, always would be. He remembered the last woman. Rage roiled inside him still. If Sophia hadn't made him so damn mad and crossed him—

Catching the anger, he took a deep breath and tamped it down. Sophia was dead and gone. This woman was here and now, and he needed her help.

His leg still throbbed, and he saw that his pant leg had been cut away and the wound on his thigh bandaged. "What day is it?" he asked as his eyes scanned the run-down inside of the trailer with its battered and scraped metal cabinets, godawful orange-and-gold sofa, and two dinette chairs that looked as if they'd been stolen from the sixties. The stuffing was leaking out of their gray vinyl backs. But the place looked clean, and he thought he smelled something cooking.

"It's Friday. Around midnight."

He'd lost two days! Still, he was alive and apparently getting better. Even though he hated the idea, he needed this woman—for lots of reasons. If he was going to win her over, he had to start now. Before he could, he heard a meow behind him.

"That's Fluffy," the woman told him. "She's real friendly. You like cats? I've got three of them, or they got me."

He hated cats. But this woman obviously took in strays and he might as well take advantage of that. "Sure. I like them just fine." He tried to hike himself up against the arm of the couch but the cloth fell from his burning forehead and his head throbbed along with his leg.

"Jeez, I feel like sh—" He stopped abruptly. "How did you get me in here? Last thing I remember I was standing outside."

"I'm stronger than I look."

Time to start getting under her skin. "I guess you are," he said, and then gave her one of his best shy smiles. "What made you help a stranger?"

She shrugged. "You needed help and you still do. Your leg is infected. It was a bullet that did that, wasn't it?"

He could out-and-out lie and probably make it convincing, but sometimes half-truths were better than whole ones. If he won her over to his side, maybe he'd have the ace he needed. "Do you want the truth?"

She nodded.

"You might want to throw me out, or grab up your valuables and take off with your cats when I tell you." He knew he had to look like hell but her gaze passed slowly over his red-brown hair, the planes of his face, his muscled body, as if he was the most handsome man on earth.

She shook her head. "I'm not going nowhere."

Something had made this woman survive whatever type of life that had put those lines on her face and had pushed her to live out here in this rusty old trailer in poverty. He could use that strength and survival instinct to his benefit. "How did you know it was a bullet?"

"I've seen it before. My brother got in trouble with other kids—and with the law."

He didn't care about her brother, but he wanted her sympathy and he bet he'd get it if he acted like he was interested. "Where's your brother now?"

"Don't know. Took off last time he was paroled. Haven't seen him in about three years."

"That's rough," Clint responded empathetically,

if not sincerely. "Is he the only family you have?" He had to know if there was a chance her relatives would be in and out of this place.

"Yep. No one else."

Clint smiled at her again. "No boyfriends?"

She blushed. "I don't have money for clothes and such that would get them to look at me."

"A good man sees beneath the clothes." It was easy to tell women what they wanted to hear.

Her cheeks grew even pinker. "You were going to tell me your story," she said as if she was eager to hear it.

"First, tell me your name."

"Betsy. Betsy Keene."

Although his body felt as if it never wanted to move again, he stretched out his hand to her and took a gamble. "My name's Clint. Clint Lockhart."

Surprise flashed in her eyes, but before she could pull away he said, "A rich man framed me for murder. He hates my guts and made sure they sent me to prison for life. But I'm no murderer, Betsy. Honest, I'm not."

He slowly pulled away, then leaned back against the sofa arm, feeling weaker than he'd ever felt in his life and resenting it. He had to convince her to help him and wondered how much she'd heard or read. "What do you know about me?"

"Not much. Just what I heard at the diner where I work. They said you killed Sophia Fortune, then the judge sent you to prison. How did you get out?"

At least she wasn't running or calling the cops, and she looked more interested than afraid. "They were transferring me to another prison because of over-crowding," he answered, watching her eyes. "The van was in an accident. I managed to get free, and took off. One of the guards shot at me and, well, here I am." He looked at her through half-closed lashes. "I desperately need your help."

After a moment's hesitation she said, "I took you in because you needed help, and I know how people get railroaded. My brother did."

He covered her hand with his, though it took a determined effort. "Betsy, I swear I *was* railroaded. Do you believe me?"

After studying him for a few moments, she nodded.

Being handsome went a long way. "I can't go to a doctor," he said, still gazing into her eyes as if she was the most beautiful woman on earth.

"I know. I cleaned your leg out as best I could while you were out."

"I don't know how to thank you." He kept his voice low and husky. Her hand was still under his and he gave it a tender squeeze, then let his thumb gently stroke her wrist as he pulled away. He could tell she was affected by it. Her eyes became all soft and she bit her lower lip.

"Will you help me, Betsy?"

She didn't take long to think about it, then she nodded again. Finally she motioned to the stove. "I brought home some bones from the diner to make broth. You gotta keep drinking. If we can break your fever, you'll be okay. But I don't know how soon it will be till you can walk on that leg. Could be a couple weeks, even."

The way the leg felt, the way *he* felt, he knew she could be right.

The effort of this conversation had cost him. His mouth was dry and he felt dizzy again.

She took the cloth from where it had fallen to his waist. "I'll make this cold again and get you something to eat, then you can rest. That's what you need, you know. Lots of rest."

He needed a hell of a lot more than rest but, for now, rest and Betsy Keene would have to do.

As Reed rambled about the adobe late Sunday afternoon, he was amazed at how empty it felt without Mallory in it. Yet when she was here, she warily kept her distance and, he had to admit, so did he. This afternoon she'd told him she was going up to the "big house," as she called it, to help Rosita and Lily get ready for the barbecue. Checking his watch, he realized he should head up there, but there was something else he had to do first. It would be almost 8:00 a.m. in Sydney.

He picked up the telephone and dialed his home. It rang about eight times, and he was almost ready to give up when he heard, "Crown Peak, Brody Fortune here."

At age thirty, Brody was six years younger than Reed. He was a businessman through and through and handled all the financial aspects of the Crown Peak Ranch. When he came to Texas, he would be arranging the merger between his family's business and their uncle Ryan's company.

"Are you packed yet?" Reed asked, knowing his brother would recognize his voice.

"Packed? I'm not leaving for twelve days. How's it going over there, anyway?"

"Something's come up."

"Like?" Brody prompted.

"I got married."

Shocked silence met his announcement. "Did Stephanie join you there?" Brody asked, puzzled.

Reed closed his eyes for a moment, knowing his brother wasn't going to understand this because he didn't himself. "Stephanie broke off the engagement last week and I married someone else." This silence went longer than Reed expected, and finally in frustration he asked, "Are Mom or Dad around?"

"No. No one is. Matilda wanted to go into Sydney and, of course, Griff wouldn't let her go alone. He'll make her behave whether she wants to or not," Brody said absently. "He just came back from another one of his vanishing acts."

"He's still coming to the U.S., isn't he?" Reed knew he couldn't distract his brother for long, but he could try.

"Yes, to keep an eye on all of us. You know Griff."

Reed's mom and dad had adopted Griff. They'd found him sleeping under a bush on the ranch, filthy, his clothes ragged. He was around seven at the time. He'd been badly beaten and wouldn't speak. All of them had given him love and a place in their family, and he had no memory of what had happened to him and no knowledge of his previous life. But it had scarred him. He was a loner, yet his loyalty to his family and his love for them was unquestionable and undeniable.

Brody went on. "And Mom and Dad and Max and Christopher went to look at horses. They won't be back until tomorrow. So that means I'm the only one you need to explain this to right now. Just who did you marry?"

"Her name's Mallory Prescott. Her half brother works for Ryan."

"You couldn't wait till we arrived to get married? Maybe Mom and Dad would have even come."

"It was an impulse."

"You're adventurous, Reed. You're not impulsive. What's going on?"

Brody probably knew him better than anyone else. "I'll explain when you get here."

"The reason you can't explain now is..."

"It's complicated."

"I should have guessed," Brody muttered. "As complicated as these missions Griff goes on that require secrecy. Do you think I'm going to be able to explain this to him and everyone else without them having scores of questions?"

"Just tell them you don't know the details...because you don't."

There was a pause, then his brother asked, "So, what's she like, can you tell me that?"

"She's beautiful and sweet but so exasperating sometimes—" He stopped.

Brody laughed. "I hope that means she's a lot more spirited than Stephanie was."

"Spirited is probably a good word to describe her."

"Is she from Texas?"

"No, San Francisco. Why do you ask?"

"There's something about that soft Texas accent on a woman..."

"What do you know about Texas women? You've never been here."

"I knew a woman from Texas when I was in college."

Brody had gone to Winslow College outside of Sydney. "Was she an exchange student?"

"Yes, and since I'll be in Texas while I get this merger settled, I'd like to try to find her."

Reed remembered a few months when Brody had been in college but hadn't been his usual steady self. He'd let his grades slide. He hadn't bothered to shave, and he'd moped around looking almost as lonely as Griff did sometimes, growling at anyone who talked to him. He wouldn't tell them what was wrong. But finally he'd snapped out of it. Could it have had something to do with this girl?

"I'll help you however I can," Reed offered. "With Ryan's connections he can probably find her quickly, if that's what you want."

"I'll figure out what I want when I get there. In the meantime, you know one of the family is going to call you and try to get more information than you gave me. Be prepared."

Reed thought about his brother's words as he put on a fresh shirt and drove up to Lily and Ryan's. He always tried to be prepared when he was hiking through the desert or exploring Australia's rain forest. But since Mallory came into his life…

How could he be prepared to answer questions when he wasn't sure what was going on himself?

There were cars and trucks parked everywhere, from the stables to the garages as well as in front of the house. Rosita met Reed at the door. "Your wife is a good helper. I don't know what I would have done without her this afternoon."

"How did she help?"

"A little of this, a little of that. She arranged roses for centerpieces, helped set up the buffet, decorated baskets to hold the *cascarónes*."

"What are they?"

"A *cascarón* is a confetti-filled eggshell. You break it over the head of someone you love or care about to bring them good luck."

"I'll remember that," he said with a smile.

Going through the great room into the courtyard, Reed found Mallory in the thick of the activity. Early this morning the caterers had brought a smokehouse and set it up behind the garages. Now they were filling the buffet table with ribs and brisket and other dishes. Mallory stood talking with Ryan, Dallas and Cruz, laughing over something one of them had said. She'd obviously gone back to the cabin and changed before he'd returned from the barn because instead of shorts, she was wearing a white peasant blouse and a red-flowered skirt that practically dipped to her ankles. The lace edging skimmed her sandals. As always when he saw her, a rush of adrenaline surged through him. But he kept his expression neutral as he walked toward her, waving to a group of cowhands he knew, as well as noting couples and strangers who were Ryan and Lily's friends and neighbors.

When Ryan saw Reed, he smiled broadly. "Mallory's been telling us about your evening in San Antonio. Maybe Lily and I will have to go with you the next time. It's been a long time since I saw the sights from one of those river barges."

Reed moved close beside Mallory and circled her waist with his arm. She stood perfectly still.

Suddenly, Ryan clapped his hands loudly and called, "Everyone, can I have your attention, please?

Please pick up a drink so you can join me in a toast.'' A waitress brought a tray of champagne glasses and offered one to both Mallory and Reed. The others already had glasses in their hands.

Mallory picked up the glass with a quick look at Reed, and he knew she wasn't about to drink it.

Raising his glass, Ryan nodded to Reed and Mallory. ''I'd like to present to you Mr. and Mrs. Reed Fortune, our most recent newlyweds. Reed and Mallory, these are our friends and neighbors, and we hope you get to know them all. But for now, I want to wish you a long, healthy and happy marriage filled with blessings too numerous to count.''

A couple of the cowhands let out whoops of agreement and everyone lifted their glasses, then took a sip, toasting the bride and groom.

There was no doubt that Mallory was embarrassed but Reed knew they had to play this out. Turning her toward him, he bent his head and kissed her. The instant their lips touched, the banked fire between them leaped high and bright. His tongue touched hers, and she responded with a low moan. He would have kept kissing her, but suddenly someone was beside him and he heard a noise above their heads. Breaking the kiss, he felt something falling onto his hair and down his face.

Zane was grinning at them, holding colorful cracked eggs above their heads. The shells fell along with the confetti from their hair to their shoulders to the ground. ''An old custom to wish you good luck,'' Zane explained, his eyes twinkling.

Mallory murmured, ''Thank you, Zane,'' and brushed the confetti from her cheeks and her shoulders. Reed helped her, but when his fingers grazed the skin at her throat, he felt the tremor go through her and their gazes met. He saw the lingering effects from the kiss still in her eyes, and he wondered how long they could deny the fire between them without getting burned by it.

Rosita rang a small bell at one end of the table. ''It's time to eat, and there's a lot here, so you better get started.''

The buffet line moved along quickly. With plates full, Reed guided Mallory toward a table where Cruz and Savannah, Mary Ellen and Sam Waterman sat. After introducing Mallory to Mary Ellen and Sam, the two women started chatting amicably. If Mallory had questions about Mary Ellen's relationship to her brother Clint, she didn't voice them. It was easy to see that Mary Ellen was loved by all the Fortunes, and she loved them.

Partway through the meal, musicians began playing. Cruz explained to Reed and Mallory that the music was Tejano, a rhythmic Tex-Mex, country-western style. The beat was lively and after finishing their meals, Cruz and Savannah, as well as Sam and Mary Ellen, excused themselves to dance with other couples around the fountain.

There had been a long table specifically set up for all the children. Rosita and Gwen had manned it, but now the boys and girls ran and played in the midst of everyone else.

Reed watched Mallory as she seemed to be trying to absorb it all. ''So what do you think of the Texas barbecue?'' he asked her.

''I think it's wonderful. Ryan and Lily seem to embrace everyone they know and make them part of their family. I've never experienced anything like it.''

"I guess when you come from a large family like I do, you take it all for granted. I know I can depend on my brothers and Matilda no matter what, and they know they can depend on me."

"You're very fortunate to be part of all this."

"You're part of it now, too." He meant as his wife, but knew she wouldn't accept that explanation. "Ryan and Lily treat Dawson as a son. You're going to be welcome here anytime."

Before Mallory could respond, Hank came up to them and slapped Reed on the back. "Enjoying yourselves?" Hank had been a cowhand on the Double Crown since he'd landed here in his late twenties. He knew everything there was to know about the horses, cows, and the land, as well as the Fortune family.

"Great barbecue. I guess you've seen a lot of them," Reed remarked.

"At least one every summer for more years than I want to count. Mallory, I was watching you today as you were helping Rosita. You fit in right well." Hank grinned at Reed. "You picked a great replacement filly and right quick, too. Must have been meant."

The hurt look on Mallory's face stabbed Reed, but before he could try to smooth things over, she hopped up from the table, saying, "There's something I have to get inside."

Tears pricked at Mallory's eyes as she weaved her way through the people in the courtyard, telling herself she shouldn't be upset, telling herself that Hank had only spoken the truth. After all, she and Reed only had a "pretend" marriage, so why should she care? But she did.

Once in the great room, she took a few deep breaths. The air-conditioning cooled her but as she brushed her hair away from her face, pieces of confetti floated from it and she remembered all the wishes of good luck. With a sigh, she crossed to a grouping of watercolor paintings—horses and their riders around a campfire. Life had always been fairly simple for her and it wasn't anymore. She supposed that's what happened when you started making your own decisions. Except her decision to marry Reed was still a mystery to her.

She heard the door open and close and wondered if Reed had come after her. She wasn't sure what she'd say to him if he had. But it wasn't Reed's voice she heard, it was Lily's.

"Is something wrong, Mallory?"

She knew she couldn't lie and didn't want to. "Everything happened so fast between Reed and me, I guess I'm just a little overwhelmed by it."

"You didn't look overwhelmed. You looked upset. Did you and Reed have a fight?"

"No. Someone made a remark… Sometimes I just don't understand why Reed married me. I mean he was engaged and—" She broke off, not sure how to continue.

Lily's dark eyes flashed. "Apparently Reed hasn't convinced you yet that you're not a substitute for someone else." Taking Mallory's hand, Lily pulled her to one of the sofas. As they sat, she said, "Men can be so thick sometimes."

That brought a smile to Mallory's face. "I'm sure Ryan isn't thick."

Lily laughed. "He once was, but so was I."

"Tell me about it," Mallory prompted.

Lily got a dreamy look in her eyes. "When Ryan and I met we were so young. We fell in love. It was wonderful and terrible and everything in between. But he was rich, and I felt I was just a poor girl who didn't deserve his love…that I could never be worthy of a Fortune. His brother Cameron managed to come between us and caused us to quarrel. I did something incredibly stupid and lost Ryan forever. At least, that's what I thought.''

''What happened then?'' Mallory asked.

''I moved away, married someone I had dated before Ryan but didn't really love, and forged a life for myself. But I never forgot Ryan or the bond between us, or his love and his respect. I had been a widow for ten years when I saw him again, and it was as if we'd never been apart. But this time no obstacle could come between us. Not even me being accused of his wife's murder.'' Lily patted Mallory's knee. ''When you meet your true love, Mallory, that love lasts forever. Don't ever doubt that.''

Mallory had listened to everything Lily had said, but one fact stood out sharp and clear. Lily and Ryan had fallen in love and had never forgotten that love. True love, only love, forever love. Just as her mother had told her. The fact that Reed would probably never forget Stephanie sat like a lead weight on Mallory's heart.

The French doors opened and Reed stepped inside. ''I thought my wife might like to dance a waltz.''

He used ''wife'' so easily, as if it were true, but they both knew better. Sometimes she forgot why they were going on with this charade, then she remembered. Winston. Forcing a smile, she stood and crossed to Reed. ''I haven't waltzed in a long time.''

''I'll refresh your memory.''

Remembering their dances at the Golden Spur, an

anticipatory quiver went through her. As he held the door open, she preceded him outside. Many couples were dancing to the button accordion's music. Reed found an empty spot and took her into his arms, but today they danced in the standard position with space between them.

He gazed down at her and said, "Hank didn't mean anything by his remark."

"It's what everyone is thinking," she murmured.

"You don't know that."

"It's what *I'm* thinking."

Reed's blue eyes studied her. "We shouldn't have to do this much longer."

The strength of his arms around her, the set of his jaw, the lock of hair falling casually over his forehead, all made her long for something that seemed much too far from her grasp. Being close to him hurt. She didn't know why, and she had to figure it out. She couldn't do that with him holding her. With him looking at her. With him dancing with her.

Her feet stopped moving and she pulled away from him. Keeping her voice low, she said, "Winston doesn't have spies here, and I can't do this right now. There are enough people that we can mingle and talk without anyone noticing we're not together." Leaving his arms, she went to help Rosita refill platters.

Reed couldn't take his eyes off Mallory the rest of the evening. She'd been right. There *were* enough people here that no one noticed that they weren't standing together or talking together or pretending to be newlyweds. She was feeling trapped again, he could tell, and he wouldn't be surprised if she wanted to take off before Dawson returned.

But he wouldn't let her. Men such as Winston

didn't quit. He was just biding his time until he made his next move.

Above all else, he was going to protect Mallory from Winston. But he had to admit he wanted a lot more than to simply keep her safe. Some kind of bond had formed between them, and each day it grew stronger. It was based on desire, but there was more, too. More that he didn't understand. More that had to do with his engagement to Stephanie and how he'd almost forgotten about the dream he'd once had with her. Now his dreams seemed to be filled with Mallory.

Reed was sitting with a group of men in the great room later that evening, only half listening to the conversation, when Mallory came in looking for him. She came up to him with a smile, but he knew the smile wasn't genuine. He was beginning to be able to tell a lot of things about her.

"I'm going to go back to the cabin," she told him. "If you want to stay longer, that's fine. Cruz and Savannah can give me a ride."

Standing, he said, "I'll take you back." His voice brooked no argument.

After they made their rounds of goodbyes, they drove back in silence. As they entered the cabin, the ceiling fan drew the night breeze with all its scents and sounds in through the windows.

"Cruz and Hank said it's fine with them if you want to work with the colts again tomorrow." Reed felt he had to break the tension before she went and hid in the bedroom. Conversation concerning something she cared about might do it.

"Is it fine with you, too?"

There was something in her voice, a bit of rebellion that rankled. "Mallory, I don't control your every move."

"Sometimes it seems like it. There's a fine line between being protected and being a prisoner."

The tension and frustration that had been niggling at him erupted. "You know, Mallory, you're a spoiled little rich girl who wants everything her own way. Maybe you'd better grow up and take a good look at reality when it hits you in the face. If you'd rather be back in San Francisco with Winston Bentley, you're free to go. I won't stop you."

"You know that's not what I want," she said softly, looking hurt.

"Then I guess you're just going to have to make the best of a difficult situation."

Her shoulders straightened, and he knew he'd set a match to her rebelliousness. "I do intend to make the best of it." Her chin lifted. "Tomorrow morning I'm meeting with Lily to discuss redecorating a suite of rooms. Tomorrow afternoon I'll help with the horses, and tomorrow night, I'm going to create a plan for my life. I don't need to wait until Dawson returns to consult with a real estate agent about shop space, or to call a few furniture stores and find out if they need an interior decorator to help with their clients. I'm going to put my life in order, Reed. Very soon you won't have to worry about protecting me."

With that announcement, she turned and went into the bedroom, and Reed knew he wouldn't see her anymore tonight. She could be so damn frustrating that he felt like putting his fist through the wall. Sucking in a deep breath and some controlled patience, he knew he'd be better off coming up with a plan to take the edge off of Mallory's restlessness.

A good night's sleep would help.

But as he unfolded the sofa and he could still smell the scent of her lingering perfume, he doubted whether a good night's sleep was any more likely than finding relief from the relentless desire he felt for Mallory Prescott.

Eight

Around midnight on Sunday, Clint restlessly paged through a week-old tabloid Betsy had brought in. There was nothing in it he wanted to read, but he didn't have anything else to do with her waitressing at a twenty-four-hour diner and his thigh still burning like the fires of hell. But his fever had broken this morning, and he was grateful for that. Maybe now he could build up his strength and get back on his feet.

He hated being an invalid, beholden to someone else. He already had Betsy under his spell. He could tell. When he smiled at her, she was by his side with a damp cloth or a glass of water or a cup of broth. But, hell, he needed real food and new clothes and a plan. If he could get to the cash and fake ID stashed in his cabin on the Double Crown... He had to convince Betsy to stick her neck out and go get it for him.

When he heard the sputtering of her old car, he knew it wouldn't take much to convince her. All he had to do was to give her a piece of a dream.

She stepped inside, and two cats followed her. Clint guessed why. She was carrying a plastic box with something wrapped in tinfoil on top of it.

''Sorry I'm late, but I had a chance to pick up extra

tips. I wasn't goin' to turn that down. How are you feelin'?''

He gave her one of his best smiles. ''Better. Thanks to you. You've taken such good care of me.''

Blushing, she pulled a chair up beside the sofa and sat. ''I brought you roast beef and mashed potatoes. They let me eat whatever I want while I'm there, and I just told them I needed something for later. Are you feelin' up to a real meal?''

''I sure am. I gotta build up my strength.''

''You're not thinking about leavin', are you?''

She looked stricken, and he knew he had a tool if he needed leverage. ''Sugar, I couldn't leave you after all you've done for me. Matter of fact, I was just thinking about how I can repay you. How would you like to be able to go to the grocery store and buy anything you want?''

''Even cat food?'' she asked, almost like a child.

''Cat food and candy bars and whatever else you want.''

''But how?''

''I told you how I was framed…that Ryan Fortune paid someone to kill his wife so he could marry his old lover.''

Betsy nodded.

''Well,'' he drawled. ''I saw it coming. He's had three wives, and the first one was my sister Janine. He made me a hired hand while they lived high on the hog, and I knew he hated my guts. Now he's turned my whole family against me. My sister, Mary Ellen, my brother Jace. I don't have anyone because of him.''

''You have me,'' Betsy said quietly.

Clint took her hand in his, knowing it was time to

take this to the next level, knowing he had to secure her complete loyalty. He brushed his thumb across the top of her hand in a caressing gesture, and the look in her eyes told him this wasn't going to be difficult at all. "You've become important to me, sugar. You saved my life and now I want to share it with you."

Betsy's heart started beating faster than it had ever beat before. For forty-three years she had waited for a man to say those kinds of things to her. When she was a teenager, she used to sneak into the movie house. She liked the stories about men and women and love and having someone the rest of your life. But men didn't look at a woman who had no pretty clothes and had no money to buy makeup. But the way Clint looked at her...she felt special. Everyone else she had ever cared about had left her. Her parents were dead, her brother far away somewhere.

The touch of Clint's fingers, the messages in his eyes, told her maybe he wanted some of the same things she did. Yet... "What if the law catches up to you?"

"We're just going to have to make sure that doesn't happen. Not until we can leave the country."

"Leave the country?"

"I'm putting together a plan. Are you with me?"

"You mean, you'd really take me with you?"

"Betsy, you've been an angel of mercy to me." Something powerful glinted in his eyes that made her feel powerful, too. "I think you could be a lot more, if that's what you want," he finished.

She wanted somebody of her own, a man of her own, so desperately that tears came to her eyes.

He lifted her hand to his lips and kissed it. "When

I'm feeling better, I'll show you just how grateful I am. But for now, if you're willing to help me out, I can make our life a little easier.''

"How can I help?''

"I need you to go to the Double Crown to the cabin where I used to live and get me something. I have cash stashed away and a few other things. Think you could do that for me?''

The idea of buying anything she wanted at a grocery store, of filling her small refrigerator, of feeding her cats, of helping this man so they could have a life together, was enough to make her say, "Just tell me what I have to do.''

For two days Mallory hardly spoke to Reed at all. Monday she'd met with Lily and shown her the ideas for the guest suite. Lily had been pleased, and they'd gone shopping today—all day—and begun the redecoration process. Mallory had bought her own jeans, boots and hat, as well. But she'd been careful how much she'd spent. Maybe she *had* been a spoiled rich kid while she was growing up, but she wasn't one now. She'd opened a checking account at a local bank and deposited the commission Lily had given her. A few more commissions and she could look for space to rent.

The tension between her and Reed since the barbecue had practically bounced off the walls. Especially when his parents had phoned last evening and insisted on giving her their good wishes. Though from the look on Reed's face during some of the conversation, they'd asked questions he was reluctant to answer. Just from their voices and their well-wishes, Mallory liked Teddy and Fiona Fortune already. They thought she'd be returning to Australia with their son. They thought she was really their daughter-in-law.

Afterward Reed had said to her, "They won't mind that I kept them in the dark when they learn your safety was involved."

But Mallory minded. She didn't like pretending to be someone she wasn't. Even more disturbing were the times she wished she and Reed weren't pretending!

As she made supper Tuesday evening, wrapping ground meat in tortillas and baking it with cheese in the oven as Rosita had instructed her to do, she heard Reed's truck pull into the drive.

When he came into the adobe and then the kitchen he remarked, "That smells good. Do I have time for a shower?"

She nodded and then said, "I called Zane this morning and got Dawson's itinerary. Then I faxed him from Ryan's office."

Reed came closer to her and she could smell leather and horses and his own scent. Steeling her senses against the pleasure of it, she went on. "I didn't want someone else telling him about our marriage. I wanted him to know what was going on before he came home."

"You told him about Bentley?"

She nodded. "As best I could in a letter. I told him no one else knows."

The nerve in Reed's jaw worked and his expression was stern. "That's quite a lot for Dawson to absorb."

"He called a little while ago and we talked. He said he'll be home on Sunday and we can hash everything out. I sensed there was something he wasn't saying— Maybe it was my imagination. Anyway, he told me I should…trust you."

"But you don't, do you?"

"I got engaged to a man who wasn't trustworthy. I can't trust my own mother to listen to me. I married you without knowing what I was doing. So I can't even trust myself! The only person I'm sure I can trust is Dawson."

In some ways she knew she *could* trust Reed, especially to keep her safe. But in others… She was afraid he'd steal her heart and go back to Australia.

Reed's body was incredibly close to hers. The two of them standing there generated more heat than the oven. She waited, almost hoping he'd kiss her, yet knowing the next kiss could lead her into more trouble than she was already in.

The silence grew almost throbbing in its intensity until he asked, "Do you think about our kisses in the middle of the night?" His voice rasped over her senses, making them more alert to him.

"Sometimes," she said in a tremulous voice, being honest, yet not completely honest. Sometimes in the middle of the night, her imagination took her much further than kisses.

"I think about them *every* night. I don't believe you've ever really been confronted by a man's physical needs, have you?"

The suppressed desire in Reed's blue eyes was something she'd never seen before, let alone known. Her throat went dry as her heart raced and she didn't think it would ever slow down again.

"How did you evade Bentley? Just say no? Tell him you had a headache?"

"Reed, don't do this—"

"Don't do what? Tell you I want you? Tell you I think you've denied your own desires and passions all your life? Let me tell you something, Mallory. Honesty and trust go hand in hand. If you had any idea of the pictures running through my mind every night, you'd know for certain you can trust me. Because I'm sure some other man would care more about his own needs than about keeping you safe. This is no picnic for me, either."

With that, he stepped away, and left her standing alone in the kitchen, her heart pounding, her body yearning for contact with his.

After he'd showered, they ate with record speed, not talking, avoiding eye contact. She had served dinner inside tonight, knowing they weren't going to linger. As Reed took his dish to the sink, he finally spoke. "I'd like to go over to see Cruz tonight, but I don't want to leave you here alone at night."

"You could drop me off at Rosita's. I want to borrow another cookbook and return this one. That way we wouldn't have to be...together."

"That might be best," he said tersely. "When will you be ready?"

"Just give me five minutes to freshen up."

He nodded. "I'll be out by the pickup."

Throughout the evening, as before, Mallory enjoyed her time with Rosita, but she couldn't help wondering what Reed was doing at Cruz's ranch, what they were discussing...if he was still feeling the aftermath of that restrained earthquake in the kitchen tonight. He was a passionate man and just the idea that he wanted her made her tremble. But why did he want her?

If that was all, it wasn't enough.

It was nearly ten-thirty when Reed returned to Rosita's for her. The night was silent except for the sound of the tires on the road as they drove home. But as he pulled onto the gravel, he ordered, "Wait here."

"Why?"

"Something's wrong. The light's on in the bedroom. You didn't turn it on before we left, did you?"

"No."

He climbed out and closed the truck door. Mallory watched as he cut across the yard to the front, but it was so dark she lost all sense of where he was. As one minute ticked by and then two, she got worried, couldn't stay in the truck, and went after him cautiously. But by the time she reached the front door, he'd turned on the living room light and its rays spilled outside.

"Reed?" she called as she opened the screen door.

"Don't touch anything," he directed.

Opening the screen, she went inside and gasped, "Oh, my."

The place was topsy-turvy. The kitchen window was broken and glass littered the floor. The cupboards stood open, sofa cushions had been tossed here and there. Even the candle and vases on the mantel had been moved. Reed stood by the phone, holding the receiver with a dish towel. "I'm calling Ryan," he said. "He needs to know about this."

Nodding, Mallory went to the bedroom. The drawers had been opened and both her clothing and Reed's were strewn across the floor along with the bed pillows and the tan spread. There didn't seem to be any rhyme or reason to the chaos.

Reed came into the bedroom. "Did you have any money tucked away in here?"

"No. My checkbook and cash were in the purse I had with me. How about you?"

"Ryan has a safe up at the house. I keep mine up there except for what I carry on me."

"Did they take anything?"

"I'm not sure this was meant to be a robbery."

"What do you mean?"

"There are three possibilities, Mallory. My first guess is Winston Bentley. He's trying to scare you, make you feel unsafe here, so you'll go running home."

"That's ridiculous."

"Is it?" Reed picked up a pair of her pink lace underwear lying on the floor. "How does it feel to come in here and know that someone has touched your things?"

Chills ran up and down her spine. Reed was right. She felt violated that someone she didn't know had gone through their things. "You said there were three possibilities."

"The second suspect would be Clint Lockhart."

The chills got worse. "You think he's here on the Double Crown?"

"There's no way of knowing. Ryan's calling the sheriff. He'll have the place dusted for prints."

"And the third possibility?" she asked, almost afraid of the answer.

"That this is a random burglar who didn't take anything because we didn't have anything he wanted. Although we have a real mess here, I can't see that anything's missing. Can you?"

Looking around, she had to agree.

By the time they'd made another cursory examination of the cabin, Ryan arrived. When he came inside, he took off his Stetson and whacked it against his thigh. "I can't believe someone managed to slip in and out of here without my security staff seeing them."

"There's something you should know," Reed said. When he cast a quick glance at her, Mallory wondered if he was going to tell Ryan that their marriage was a fake. Holding her breath, she waited.

He continued, "Mallory left an ex-fiancé back in San Francisco. A rich one who isn't too happy she married me. This could be his work."

Ryan looked from one of them to the other. "Is he that ornery?"

"Not only ornery, but dangerous. He tried to force Mallory to go back to San Francisco with him when we were in Reno. We should have told you."

Ryan was quiet for a few moments. "No use crying over spilled milk. Is anything missing?"

Both of them shook their heads.

"No real damage is done here. Whoever did this is giving us a warning. We'd better take it. I never thought I'd have to have a security system hooked up in this cabin, but that's what I'd better do. You two could come up to the house and stay—"

"I have another idea," Reed said. "Can I talk to you outside for a few minutes?"

"Sure. Excuse us, will you, Mallory?"

"Yes," she answered quickly, hoping Reed had thought of something good. The last thing they needed was to share a bedroom up at the big house.

After the men stepped outside, she paced, remembering not to touch anything. It was only a few minutes until Ryan and Reed came back in.

"I think it would be a good idea if I got you away from here for a couple of days," Reed explained, his gaze holding hers.

"Where?"

"There's a line shack about half a day's ride from the Double Crown. We could camp out a couple of nights. I could check on the herd while we're up there."

"Camp out?"

His steady blue eyes challenged her. "If you haven't slept on a bedroll under the stars at least once in your lifetime, you haven't lived."

The words he'd flung at her after they returned from the barbecue came back to haunt her. *You're a spoiled little rich girl.* Maybe she had been, and this was a gauntlet he was throwing down in front of her. She couldn't let Reed Fortune or her circumstances get the best of her. If he wanted to camp out, she'd show him that she was more than willing and very able.

"When do you want to leave?" she asked.

"Did you get everything?" Clint asked as Betsy came through the trailer door.

"Yep. The cash and the fake ID. I did just like you said. I parked way off the ranch, then followed the fence. It was scary out there in the dark with that little flashlight."

Clint knew he had to build Betsy up. He had to make her believe she could do anything—as long as she was doing it for him. "I knew you could do this for me…for us. You kept the gloves on the whole time?''

''Yep. The whole time. It was easy tonight. Nobody was in the cabin. The people staying there drove away.''

''Did the key work?''

''Nah. Like you said, they must've changed the locks. So I had to break the window. After I took the stash from under the floorboard in the bedroom, I messed everything up real good. It looked like some burglar went through it.''

The sweater Betsy wore was tattered and looked as if it had been through a war. Reaching into one of its big pockets, she took out a wad of cash and the laminated ID. ''Here you go.'' She put all of it into his lap.

''I guess you didn't find any other cash laying around?''

''Uh-uh. There wasn't much of nothin'. They're gonna think a burglar couldn't find anything worth taking. There wasn't even a TV!''

Clint wondered who was staying in the cabin now. ''So there was more than one person staying in the cabin?''

''A man and a woman.''

Usually when the Fortunes invited guests, they stayed up at the big house. Maybe they'd hired on new help. As soon as he was back on his feet, he'd find out exactly what was going on at that ranch. And he'd figure out exactly what he could do to make more trouble for Ryan Fortune than he'd ever seen.

Revenge was supposed to be sweet. Soon he'd find out just how sweet it was.

But in the meantime… He patted the couch next to his hip. "Come here, Betsy."

She perched on the sofa by his leg.

Handing her a twenty-dollar bill, he said, "You tuck that away till tomorrow, then you go buy that cat food and those candy bars."

She looked as if he'd given her the moon. After she stared down at the twenty, she glanced back up at him. "I was thinking," she said. "This couch has got to be gettin' awful lumpy. It can't be too comfortable. Maybe…" She stopped, then went on. "Maybe, you'd like to sleep in my bed tonight."

He'd suspected this invitation was coming. "I'd like that, sugar. I'd like that a lot." He reached down and flipped his hand under her hair and brought her to him for a kiss.

A man had to take what he could get. Tonight he'd take Betsy Keene and soon…he'd take down Ryan Fortune.

As Reed readied the horses the next morning, Mallory realized she might have agreed to this outing a little too quickly. Being alone with Reed, miles from civilization…

Not that it seemed as if she had anything to worry about. He'd been keeping his distance. Lots of it. They'd been up late last night until Sheriff Wyatt Grayhawk, an in-law of Ryan's, had taken a report, asked some questions and dusted the cabin for prints. Then they'd straightened up and gone to bed. Reed had convinced Ryan that they'd be fine for the few hours they were going to sleep…that he was a light sleeper and would hear any sound an intruder might make. But Ryan had insisted he put a guard on the cabin for the rest of the night to make sure they weren't disturbed. They hadn't been and soon after they'd dressed this morning Sam Waterman had arrived to do a preliminary examination for the security system Ryan wanted installed.

Reed had told Mallory there were provisions in the line shack and all they needed were bedrolls and a change of clothes. She could take her swimsuit if she wanted to go wading in the creek. Not sure exactly what they'd be doing, she packed an extra pair of jeans, socks, sneakers, shorts and a top, her swimsuit and managed to stick a towel into the bedroll. He'd eyed all of it curiously but hadn't commented as he packed saddlebags and attached their bedrolls to the back of each saddle.

Ryan himself saw them off and told them to have a good time…to try to forget about everything that had happened. But as they rode across the range, Mallory couldn't forget any of it. Not from the moment she'd awakened next to Reed, not their kisses, nor the tightrope of tension that pulled between them now. With the leather tie from her new hat swinging under her chin, she clicked to her horse and kept pace with Reed's stallion.

"Thank you for handling the subject of Winston so tactfully last night," she said, breaking the silence.

"I wasn't being tactful. I was just trying to alert Ryan to the possibility of more than one person causing trouble."

All of their conversations had been almost terse ever since those few moments in the kitchen yesterday. "But you didn't tell him that our marriage is a…sham."

After a sobering moment he muttered, "There will be time enough for that."

Again silence fell between them, and it was obvious to Mallory that Reed didn't want to talk to her. She felt like a burden, a responsibility he'd taken on and didn't really want. She didn't want to *be* his responsibility.

The countryside changed as they rode, becoming hillier. The grass grew thicker, and she could see why they brought cattle up here for summer pastures. "Have you been here before?" she asked when they stopped for a few moments to drink some water.

"My first week on the Double Crown, I drove a few head of cattle up here with another cowhand."

Again Reed made no attempt to carry on the conversation. So Mallory gave up trying. If he wanted silence, she'd give it to him.

They reached their destination in the early afternoon. The weathered shack and small corral looked like a set from an old Western. Mallory could see a stream about twenty yards behind it. Cottonwoods and cedars lined its banks. The Texas landscape in shades of brown and green stretched out behind the shack over the crest of a hill. It was a landscape that begged to be painted, and she was glad she'd tucked a small sketch pad and charcoal pencil into her saddlebag.

They rode into the corral and, as she prepared to dismount, Reed warned her, "Take care when you hit the ground. You've been on horseback a long time."

Sometimes she couldn't figure out if he was telling her what to do or looking out for her benefit. But knowing the ride *had* been a long one, she dismounted carefully. Her legs did feel like wet noodles, and she held on to the saddle for a few minutes, letting the horse prop her up.

"The circulation will come back. Shake them out."

Feeling ridiculous, she tapped one foot on the ground then the other. Reed was still watching her, and she didn't want to give him a reason to come to her rescue yet again. "I'm fine," she told him as she unhitched her saddlebag.

He dismounted easily, his boots solid on the ground. Obviously he was used to being on a horse for hours at a time. "I'll get the bedrolls if you want to go inside out of the sun."

"Reed, will you please stop telling me how to take care of myself?"

His jaw tensed and the nerve on the side of it worked. From the look in his eyes, she knew he was holding his temper and biting back a lot of things he'd like to say. Before she found out what they were, she followed his suggestion and opened the creaky door of the line shack.

The inside was Spartan—two metal cots with thin mattresses and a stand of shelves that held canned goods. A scarred rectangular table flanked by two plank-bottom chairs sat in the corner, and a cupboard stood against the far wall. Mallory laid her saddlebag on one of the cots then went to open the cupboard. She found plastic plates, silverware, mugs, pots and an assortment of biodegradable soaps—bars for bathing, liquid for dishes. On the bottom shelf she saw a stack of dishcloths, a couple of towels and packs of toilet paper.

When Reed came in, he caught her checking the

supplies. "Think you can handle this for a couple of days?"

"What's to handle?" she murmured, going over to the window and hiking it up. "We've got everything we could need." She wouldn't tell him that she was afraid of wild animals and being out in the middle of nowhere with no neighbors within shouting distance, let alone driving distance. She was also stressed out because these quarters were even smaller than the adobe's. But she told herself she'd be perfectly fine.

He motioned to the water containers next to the shelves. "Make sure you keep drinking when you're out in the sun."

Her gaze met his, and they both realized he'd just given her another order, but neither of them mentioned it, knowing it was the spark that might make the tinder ignite.

Rosita had packed them a lunch and they ate it swiftly, more to get the meal over with than to enjoy the food. Reed took a few swallows of water from his mug and set it down. "I'm going to ride out and check on the cattle this afternoon. Do you want to come along or do you want to stay here?"

She'd only slept a couple of hours last night. She was tired, and her body was already beginning to protest from the long ride. "I'll stay here." Before he could give her a warning, she added, "I won't go wandering off anywhere. I'll wait until you come back to explore."

She almost thought he was going to smile, but if the inclination crossed his mind, it never made it to his lips.

Lifting his Stetson off a peg on the wall, he set it

on his head. "I'll be back in plenty of time to get supper started."

"I can certainly open a can of beans," she muttered, seeing that there were plenty of those on the shelf.

"Maybe so, but can you start the campfire to warm them on?"

"Once you show me how, I'll be able to do it the next time," she returned with a little too much sweetness, not ready to capitulate that she needed him to take care of her.

This time the corner of his lip did twitch. "Make yourself at home," he said with a wink. Then he closed the door and was gone.

That darn sexy Australian drawl made her want to throw something at the closed door, but she simply didn't have the energy, and a few moments later she heard the clomp of hooves as Reed rode away.

Weaving in and out of the cattle, Reed checked them over superficially, his mind on Mallory. He couldn't shake her out of his head anymore. He'd lost his cool with her after the barbecue. With the cabin torn up last night, the idea that somebody might want to do her harm unnerved him so much that all he wanted to do was to hold her in his arms and keep her safe.

Well...not *all* he wanted to do.

Shadows were lengthening as he rode back to the camp, wondering what Mallory had found to occupy herself. She wasn't the type of woman who liked to sit idle. After he walked his horse the last quarter mile or so, he led Spirit into the corral and unsaddled him. The door to the shack was open, and Mallory sat at the table by the light of the window, sketching. Crossing to the table, he studied two finished scenes that she'd drawn. One was a long shot of the terrain and brush and gently sloping hills with the line shack nestled in the middle of all of it. The second was a sketch of her horse, Dusty Dawn, as he stood in the corral. She'd managed to capture his sturdiness, the alertness in his eyes, the proud set of his head.

"These are good," Reed remarked.

"Thank you. It's a hobby, and it comes in handy when I'm working up designs or layouts."

He dumped his saddlebag at the foot of his bed. "If you want to freshen up before we eat, feel free. I'll get the campfire started."

"I'm going to take a bath, so don't worry if I'm not back in ten minutes."

The idea of her bathing in the creek put erotic pictures in his mind. "The creek water's cold."

"I'd rather be cold than dirty." Pushing back her chair, she stood and went to her bedroll, pulling out a green towel, then she took a bar of soap from the cupboard and picked up a blouse she'd laid on her bed.

He could imagine her wet, sleek with the creek water, raising her face to the last rays of the sun— "Mallory?"

She stopped at the door.

"Don't take too long or..." Or he might be tempted to join her. "Or your supper will get cold," he said curtly.

"I'll keep that in mind." She left the cabin and headed for the stream.

After Reed gathered kindling and positioned a few logs on the fire, he went to the creek to wash up before starting the rice and beans. He'd watched where Mallory had headed and chose a spot farther down. As he approached the bank, he could hear her humming and singing. Her voice was as sweet as a siren's song and if he chose to peer around the cedars, he could see her and she'd never know he was there. But *he'd* know.

If he ever saw her naked again, it would be with her consent.

She returned just as he stirred the rice and beans one last time and heated the corn muffins Rosita had sent along. Going into the cabin, she brought her bedroll out and opened it by the side of the fire, then settled on it. They ate as they watched the sun say a spectacular good-night. Every shade of pink streaked the horizon before it slipped away into darkness.

"Are you going to sleep inside the cabin or out here?" she asked.

"Out here."

"Do you mind if I sleep out here, too?"

"You're free to do whatever you want, Mallory."

"I wish," she murmured under her breath.

"If you put your mind to it, you can enjoy yourself the next couple of days." He knew she wasn't used to this kind of life and maybe bringing her here had been a mistake.

"*You* don't seem to be enjoying yourself all that much," she retorted, and stood, gathering up their dishes. "I'll take care of these since you made supper."

When she returned to the fire, she brought her sketch pad and pencil. Before long, she'd settled with her back against a rock, sketching.

As the air became damp with night dew, the distance between Reed and Mallory became more than ten feet. "I'm going to bank the fire and turn in," he said gruffly.

When she looked up and gazed at him across the fire, he saw emotions in her eyes, but he wasn't sure what they were. With his need for her increasing with every star that appeared, he wasn't going to ask any questions. He stretched out on his bedroll, his head pillowed on top of his arms. By the time Mallory took her sketch pad into the cabin and returned, he'd convinced himself he could turn off his need for her. He didn't watch her get settled but could hear every sound as she unzipped the bedroll, slid inside, then quieted.

"Good night, Mallory," he said.

"Good night."

Cattle lowed in the distance, and one of the horses softly neighed. Cicadas clicked a rhythm totally their own. The glow of the campfire hardly alleviated the inky-black night, and Reed could sense Mallory a few feet way. He didn't know how long he lay there, his eyes closed, willing himself to sleep, but he heard the call of a coyote then the rustle of Mallory's sleeping bag when she sat up. He looked over at her, but she was staring into the distance away from him.

"Mallory?"

She didn't answer, and she didn't turn around. That wasn't like her.

"What's wrong?"

But she still didn't respond, and he came to his feet, then crouched beside her. When he did, he could see she was shivering. The temperature had only dropped into the upper sixties but apparently she was cold.

"Do you want to go into the cabin?"

She shook her head.

"Mallory, look at me."

When she kept her head tucked down, he lifted her chin and saw tears on her cheeks. She would have turned away from him and maybe run off, but he held her shoulders.

"Tell me what's wrong," he encouraged gently.

After a few minutes her words came out in a rush. "I don't want to need you. I don't want to depend on you." Her shoulders shook, and he suspected the past two weeks had finally caught up to her. But when he went to put his arm around her shoulder, she shied away. "And most of all," she concluded, "I don't want you to feel you have to take care of me like some lost calf. That's not what I want from a man. That's not—"

"What *do* you want from a man?" His voice was husky, because they were the only two people in the world right now and he wanted her.

When she seemed at a loss for an answer, he asked more directly, "What do you want from *me?*"

Nine

Under the slip of the moon, wide expansive black sky and twinkling white stars, Reed saw his answer in Mallory's eyes. With the embers of the fire glowing nearby, he knelt down beside her, and she rose up on her knees to meet him.

"Kiss me, Reed," she said breathlessly.

Resisting her was as out of the question as leaving her here to fend for herself. His arms encircled her and he brought her to him. His lips first tasted the salt of her tears on her cheeks but then found her mouth. He took it, demanding and possessing. She laced her fingers in his hair, and he groaned as he took her down onto the bedroll, covering her with his body. But she didn't seem to mind as his legs parted hers and their jeans created a friction hotter than nakedness.

Rolling onto his side, he took her with him. His tongue stole her breath and made it his. Kissing wasn't nearly enough as their legs intertwined and her thigh brushed where he wanted to be touched most. The need that rushed through him caused him to wonder if he'd ever known desire before. Certainly never this raging desire that could only be satisfied by Mallory. Her alluring curves were too tempting to resist, and his hands slid under the edge of her top. Her skin was so soft as he pressed their lower bodies together harder, imagining the feel of her skin against his. His thumb teased her nipple through her bra, and she moaned. Every sound she made raised the height of his arousal…the intensity of the passion he'd first felt at the Golden Spur.

Quickly he reached around her and unfastened her bra. As his hand cupped her breast and she arched against it, he knew it wouldn't take much to catapult him over the edge. But she was a virgin.

A virgin.

He had to be sure that what they were about to do was the right thing for both of them. Breaking the kiss, he stroked her cheek. "Mallory, if we…" he hesitated only a moment "…have sex, we won't be able to get an annulment."

The word annulment took the stars from her eyes and the blush from her cheeks. "No," she said softly, "I guess we won't." She started to roll away from him. "I'm sorry, Reed. I—"

Taking a deep breath himself, he finally said, "There's nothing to be sorry about." Then he thought about why he'd come to her in the first place. "Are you scared out here?"

Her silence was telling.

Smoothing her bedroll out under him, he held out his arm to her. "Come here."

She looked unsure.

"Come on," he prompted. "We're going to count the stars and fall asleep."

"Are you sure? I mean…"

"Neither of us got very much sleep last night. I bet before you get to one hundred you'll be snoring."

"I don't snore," she responded indignantly.

He laughed. "Okay, you'll be sleeping silently like the lady you are." It felt good to be teasing her again.

Smiling at him now, she moved closer. When her hip grazed his, she awkwardly moved away again, but he pulled her to his shoulder and said, "Relax." He was still aroused but there was a peacefulness in holding her that created a satisfaction he'd never quite known before. When she finally relaxed against him, he turned his face toward her and inhaled the scent of her hair. Then he looked straight up at the sky and started counting. Soon he felt the slower rhythm of her breathing and knew she'd fallen asleep. With her tucked against him, he closed his eyes and fell into a welcome slumber.

It was midafternoon on Saturday when Mallory and Reed rode past the largest corral on the Double Crown. Although a tingling tension had remained between them since their night under the stars, they'd also formed a bond, and she had to acknowledge to herself that she was falling in love with Reed Fortune.

The past two nights they'd lain side by side, rather than together, counting stars…and talking—about anything and everything. He'd described the opal mines where he'd worked one summer while he was in college. The stars always reminded him of opals, he'd said. She'd understood exactly what he'd meant and confided in him how as a child, she'd go into her mother's room, open her jewelry box and just appreciate the beauty of everything inside—the colors, the stones catching the light. She'd told him about her first client when she'd signed on for her apprenticeship and how nervous she'd felt. He'd admitted that

when he was a child, being one of six children sometimes made him feel lost in a crowd, but he wouldn't
have had it any other way.

It had been so easy discussing horses and family
and anything else that had come into their heads.
Anything, that is, but how they felt about being together…about each other.

Mallory knew she was headed for heartache. This
was an impossible situation. Reed had been engaged
to another woman a little over two weeks ago. She'd
walked away and he'd been left with his feelings.
Love didn't diminish or end simply because you
wanted it to. Besides, he was going back to Australia
at the end of the summer. She was courting disaster
to let her feelings get any more entwined around him.
But she couldn't seem to help herself. There was
something about this man that she admired and respected…and needed. That's what bothered her most.

She'd almost hated to return to the Double Crown.
While Reed had tended cattle and mended fences,
she'd ridden out with him and sat under a tree,
sketching. She'd done lots of charcoal sketches of
him and the horses and scenery, but mostly of Reed.
Returning to the ranch today brought back the reasons why they'd left—the threat of Winston and
maybe Clint Lockhart. She'd be moving out of the
cabin tomorrow and going to live with Dawson. Part
of her resisted that move, too.

As she looked toward the barn, she saw Hank
standing outside the stall doors with someone. A man
in a suit. Suddenly she realized who it was. Reining
in her horse, she jumped off and ran toward Dawson.
He gathered her in a huge bear hug.

A few moments later, leaning back, she studied

him. At thirty-two, Dawson looked every bit the con-
servative businessman, from the cut of his light
brown hair to the fine quality of his suit. He was well-
built and almost as broad-shouldered as Reed. There
was affection in his hazel-green eyes.

"What are you doing here? I didn't think you'd
be back until tomorrow," she said, glad he'd returned
early, yet also realizing that meant she'd be leaving
Reed.

"I managed to tie everything up a day early."

Hank moved away to give them some privacy as
Reed brought their horses to the barn. "Hi, mate,"
he greeted Dawson.

But Dawson just scowled at him. "I don't know
whether to congratulate you or make you explain everything that happened in Reno."

"Her fiancé tried to kidnap her and I stopped
him," Reed said succinctly.

"You had to marry her to do that?"

"Is that what she told you?" Reed asked.

"Don't talk about me as if I'm not here," Mallory
protested. "I told Dawson—" She looked at Reed.
"I didn't want to go into the Golden Spur and the
champagne in a fax or over the phone—"

"So, why *did* the two of you get married?" her
brother asked, looking from one to the other.

"I'd had too much champagne and Reed, well…"
She threw up her hands embarrassed by the entire
scenario. "Look, Dawson, it doesn't matter. The
point is—now you're back so we can file for an annulment or whatever we have to do."

"But you've been living together. You mean to
tell me that you haven't…"

Her cheeks were burning and she was glad she

didn't have to explain this to anyone else. "No, we haven't. We only stayed married because of Winston. But if I can just move in with you until I can afford a place of my own, Reed can get back to his life and I can start mine."

Dawson shook his head. "That's the problem. You can't stay with me."

She'd never thought Dawson would turn her away. They didn't know each other very well, but there had always been this connection between them. Her face must have shown her disappointment.

"Not because I don't want you there, Mallory," Dawson explained. "I wasn't sure when we talked, but yesterday I finalized my schedule for the next few weeks. I have to go out of town again. During the next month I'll be gone more than I'm home. That's no protection for you. I suppose you could get a restraining order against Bentley...."

"That won't protect her against him. We'll have to keep pretending we have a real marriage," Reed concluded.

Dawson eyed them both. "Mallory, are you agreeable to that? I'm flying out again Monday morning and other than taking you with me, I don't have another solution."

The idea that he'd actually take her with him warmed her heart. "I could stay at your apartment and keep the door locked until you return."

"As if you'd do that," Reed muttered with a hard look at her.

"You'd prefer being locked in my apartment to staying with Reed?" Dawson asked.

"No, of course not, but I'm sure Reed's tired of my being around."

"I never said that." He had a stubborn set to his chin.

If she stayed, she'd fall deeper in love with him. Both men were waiting for her to make a decision. "All right, I'll stay with Reed."

"Good," Dawson concluded. "Then I'll know you'll be safe. Ryan told me about Clint Lockhart and the security system he had installed at the cabin. It's state of the art."

"No word on Lockhart yet?" Reed asked.

Dawson shook his head. "Are you tired from your camping, or do you want to see some of the sights?" he asked Mallory. "Like I said, I'm free till Monday morning."

"I'd love to see some of the missions and the Alamo."

"That's easily done. Reed, are you going to join us?" Dawson asked.

"No, I have to become familiar with the security system and check on some mares I've been following."

"You can meet us in town for dinner." Dawson extended the invitation, obviously meaning it.

But Reed shook his head. "I know Mallory would like to spend some time with you. Go ahead and take it. I have plenty to keep me occupied."

"Are you coming back to the cabin now?" Mallory asked Reed. The bond that had formed while they were gone seemed to be breaking now that they were back. She could feel distance again, yet she knew that was probably for the best.

"Not right now, but I'll be there when you get home tonight."

"I'll make sure I deliver her safe and sound to you," Dawson said with a grin.

Mallory sighed. One man protecting her was bad enough, now she had two.

Although Reed had kept busy all day, as the time neared midnight he paced the living room. He knew Mallory was safe with Dawson. Still....

At the sound of Dawson's car, he breathed a sigh of relief. He heard her call goodbye and then she opened the door. She stopped when she saw him standing there. "I thought you might have gone to bed."

"I didn't want to turn on the security system until after you came in."

"Oh," she said softly. She was wearing white shorts and a red top and sneakers, and she'd never looked more attractive.

"Did you get reacquainted?"

Her gaze passed over his bare chest, then his sleeping shorts, and he could feel the heat from it.

Stepping away from him, she laid her purse on the table. "Yes, we did. We talked in a way we never had a chance to before."

"About anything in particular?"

She didn't say anything immediately, then answered, "About our parents. I never realized how deeply Dawson was affected by our father leaving his mother to marry my mother. He felt betrayed for himself and his mother, and her bitterness throughout the years didn't help. She's still bitter. I'm amazed that Dawson doesn't resent me and that somehow he stayed untouched by it."

"Untouched? I doubt that. But maybe he had the strength of character to rise above it."

She seemed to think about that.

"Are you spending time with him tomorrow?" Reed asked.

"He's going to pick me up early. We're going to play tennis at his apartment complex, then go to some museums, see more sights. I really do love San Antonio."

The city was as vibrantly alive as Mallory herself, and Reed should have known she'd fit right in. Going to the wall, he turned on the security system, then went and sat on the edge of the open sofa bed. "I'm going to turn in. If I'm gone before you get up tomorrow morning, you have a good time."

"I will," she said softly.

There didn't seem to be anything else to say. When Mallory went into the bedroom, he settled on the sofa bed, thinking about their nights under the stars and wishing that's where they were right now.

Introducing a halter to the filly for the first time took all of Mallory's concentration on Monday afternoon. She spoke softly to the horse, touching her gently. Finally she slipped on the halter. The filly shook her head a few times. Then Mallory slipped it back off, knowing they had worked enough for one afternoon. Leading the filly into the yearling pasture, she let her run free. Ears alert, tail flying, the young horse cavorted through the grass, meeting up with another filly.

Mallory headed back to the corral, thinking about Dawson and the wonderful day she'd had with him yesterday. They'd played tennis in the morning at his apartment complex. He had a great place, and he'd shown her the guest room where she could stay when he was back in San Antonio on a consistent basis. They'd gone out for lunch, toured a museum and visited another mission. Somehow he'd gotten tickets to a play, and she'd arrived back at the cabin around eleven-thirty.

But before she'd said goodbye to Dawson, he'd asked her a question. *Why did you marry Reed?* His expression had been serious, and she'd known he'd wanted the truth, not a flippant answer. So she'd explained the best she could what had happened and told him she didn't remember the marriage ceremony. He'd studied her then, and in the shadows of the car had said, "Maybe your heart did something your logic would never let you do."

Was that possible? Had she fallen in love with Reed the night she'd met him?

Reed had been waiting up for her again, and they'd spoken briefly about their plans for today. But she'd remembered all too well what had almost happened under the stars and moonlight up at the line shack. They avoided getting too close to each other as if an inadvertent touch or a brush of skin would tip the scales and they'd fall into a passion that would only complicate their lives even more.

As Mallory approached the training arena, she spotted a truck and trailer parked not far from the airplane hangar door. Hearing voices, she went inside thinking Reed had probably come in here to get out of the hot sun.

A man wearing a gray Stetson and looking about the same age as Reed was standing in the center of the arena with Reed and a little girl who couldn't have been more than ten. Sticking close to the man's side, the little girl seemed to be afraid of the chestnut mare that Reed held the reins to. The man was telling Reed, "Carrie's not used to horses. We lived in town until about a month ago when I finally bought a place with some land. That's why I called Mr. Fortune. I wanted a horse that would be easy for her to handle."

"This mare's as gentle as they come," Reed responded. He crouched to Carrie's eye level. "Her name's Nita, and she's just waiting for you to get to know her."

Carrie didn't look convinced.

With a gentle smile Reed asked, "Can you tell me what you're afraid of?"

"She's so big."

He didn't laugh at the little girl, but nodded in agreement. "Yes, she is. Much bigger than you. But if you really get to know her, she can become one of your best friends. Then she won't seem so big at all. When you're riding her, it will seem as if you're ten feet tall. If you learn how to act around her and what to do, it won't matter that she's so big."

Stepping away from her father just slightly, Carrie asked Reed, "Can I pet her?"

He straightened. "Sure, you can. C'mon over here and I'll let you feel her nose. It's really soft. But you have to be very gentle so you don't frighten her."

"*Me* scare *her?*"

"She might seem big to you, but she's really very shy. If you look into her eyes, you can see that."

Mallory's chest tightened as she listened to Reed talk to the little girl and introduce her to the mare. Apparently he was as gentle and patient with children as he was with the horses, and she realized he'd make a wonderful father.

She didn't know how long she stood there, but eventually Carrie agreed to sit in the saddle to see how it felt. Letting Reed lift her up onto the leather, she grabbed on to the pommel. But he told her to pretend she was sitting in her favorite chair at home, a rocking chair, and then he started walking the horse slowly.

Mallory slipped out of the arena so as not to disturb them. Each day she spent with Reed she found something more to admire about him, some new strength she hadn't seen before, and she was suddenly very angry at the woman who had broken off her engagement with him so cavalierly. Was she crazy? Yet she couldn't have been. She must have had some magnificent qualities or been absolutely beautiful for Reed to have been in love with her. That thought was so upsetting that Mallory decided to stop to see if Lily was at home. They could set a date to go shopping again, and maybe she'd be able to think about something other than the man who was her husband in name only.

In no time at all, an hour had flown by as Mallory and Lily envisioned the new furniture they had ordered and the fabrics they had chosen for the suite of rooms Lily was redecorating. They made a date to go shopping to pick up decorative items, potteries, sculptures and a few scatter rugs. When Rosita called Lily to the phone, Mallory sipped iced tea in the sitting room that was part of the master suite and much cozier than the great room. A few moments later Lily returned from the bedroom, looking puzzled.

"Is something wrong?" Mallory asked.

"The florist has a delivery for you, but he said he had strict instructions to make the delivery to the cabin."

Mallory rose to her feet. "Maybe Dawson sent them to surprise me."

"Or Reed," Lily suggested with a wink.

Only in her dreams, Mallory thought. "Is the delivery person there now?"

"Yes, he said he'd wait for you."

After Mallory confirmed the time she'd meet Lily to go shopping on Tuesday, she hurried and drove to the adobe. A large delivery truck sat out front. She parked and took out her new key, opened the door and flicked off the security alarm. The delivery man, who looked to be in his twenties, carried a box of long-stemmed roses, she supposed, and a huge arrangement of tiny orchids and ferns.

"Two?" she asked when he came to the door.

"A lot more than two, ma'am. I've got a whole truckful."

Mallory suspected the worst as he brought the flowers inside. As he went back to the truck, she took the lid from the roses, beautiful red ones, and picked up the card that lay on top of the tissue.

Mallory—
Just a reminder that I'm waiting for you. All of them remind me of your beauty and sweetness.
                              Always,
                              Winston

Mallory's heart sank as the delivery man brought bouquet after bouquet into the adobe. There were ordinary flowers such as carnations and daisies, but then there were some beautiful delicate ones in unusual colors that she knew must be exotic. At least fifteen bouquets filled the cabin with their rich fragrance and beauty. After tipping the young man, she put her hands on her hips and looked around.

Winston apparently thought he could flatter her and buy her, making her forget what he'd tried to do. Well, she wasn't about to forget, and she knew he wasn't the type of man she wanted to marry. Not with her feelings for Reed growing so strong. Not with her respect and admiration for him mounting every day. She wished she could send the flowers back to Winston, but that was impossible. She needed to think about what to do next. Donate the flowers to a hospital, for one thing. Deciding what to do about Winston was another. Maybe if she got a shower and then made supper, a brilliant idea would come to her and she could convince Winston they needed to go their separate ways.

Quitting a little earlier than usual, Reed had decided to ask Mallory to go out to dinner with him. Hopefully she hadn't started supper yet. If she had, afterward, they could go for a ride. Unlocking the door, he was glad to see she was using her common sense and keeping the adobe secure. But as he stepped inside, the scent of flowers hit him and he saw the many bouquets. He almost forgot to switch off the security alarm, but he flipped it just in the nick of time. A knot twisted in his stomach as he went toward one of the bouquets and lifted out the card, which read, "Always, Winston." Bouquet after bouquet had the same card placed in it.

Reed swore long and hard, jealousy ripping his

gut. Could Bentley win her back? He was good-looking in a polished sort of way. He apparently knew how to overwhelm a woman, and Mallory *had* said yes to his marriage proposal.

She didn't even remember *their* marriage ceremony in Reno. Sure Bentley was dangerous, but some women liked danger. Reed swore again. Just as he thought about dumping all the flowers outside, or better yet onto a manure pile, he heard the bathroom door open. Going to the bedroom, he demanded, "What the hell is all this?" He knew he shouldn't be angry with her but he was green with jealousy.

Mallory's hair was wet, and she obviously thought she'd be alone in the cabin because she was wearing only a peach towel tucked in at her breasts. The impact of her beauty wrapped around Reed and aroused him, his heart pounding harder as he waited for her explanation.

"He's trying to win me back. His card said he was waiting for me."

"And *is* he winning you back?" Reed asked roughly.

"No! Ten roomsful of flowers won't make me forget what Winston did or what he is. He—"

Knowing he was stepping into dangerous territory, knowing he was breaching a boundary, Reed stepped closer to her. "I suppose he showered you with flowers while you were engaged?"

"Yes," she murmured.

"And gifts?"

"Yes," she murmured again.

Clasping her bare shoulders, he demanded, "Did you bring any of them with you?"

Her hazel eyes locked on his. "No, I didn't. When

I left San Francisco, I knew I was finished with Winston.''

The desire that had pulsed between them from the moment they'd met became a power greater than both of them. He could deny it no longer. Reed pulled her to him and his lips came down on hers in a hard, crushing kiss. She'd become sunlight to him, sunrise and sunset...and so many changing colors that she made his head spin. Was she truly finished with Winston Bentley IV or would he manage to call her back to him and convince her she belonged in a different life than she wanted to build here?

Reed didn't care. Not with her in his arms. Not with the sweet scent of her seeping into him. Not with her lips responding under his. Not with her hands reaching for his shoulders.

Scooping her up into his arms, he carried her to the bed where she'd lain night after night all alone. He'd wanted to go to her...seal their bodies together in an intimacy they'd never forget. Now he would make it so good for her she'd want to remember these moments forever!

He broke the kiss to gaze into her eyes again, to make sure she didn't want to run from him as she wanted to run from Bentley. ''We can't deny this, Mallory. We can't deny *us* any longer. It's too powerful.''

''Much too powerful,'' she whispered, never taking her eyes from his.

Taking that as consent, he laid her on the bed and his hand went to the place where she'd tucked in her towel. ''I want to look at you and touch you and make you tremble until you want me as much as I want you.''

When she reached up to him, she stroked his jaw, and he realized *he* was the one who was shaking. He'd never felt this way with a woman, never wanted to please her so thoroughly she'd beg for him to do it again. But Mallory was so special....

A virgin, he reminded himself once more.

He had to take this slow. He had to do it right. He had to arouse her desire until her pleasure outweighed any pain. Unfastening her towel, he brushed it away.

She was perfect. The tan on her arms was golden from her time in the sun but the rest of her body was a peach-ivory porcelain that looked almost too delicate to touch.

"Is something wrong?" she asked.

He held his breath for a moment to maintain control. "Nothing's wrong. But...has a man ever touched you before?"

"Not in the way you're going to touch me," she replied simply.

Lord, he was hotter than he wanted to be. "I should take a shower."

"You had one this morning," she said with a shy smile.

"Yes, but—"

Her fingers went to his shirt buttons and unfastened them. "I want you just the way you are."

If he'd had any thoughts of turning back, they fled. He didn't wait for her to finish unbuttoning but did it himself in record time, then stripped off his boots, socks, jeans and briefs. She was looking at him with such vulnerable innocence. He lay beside her and kissed her. When his tongue traced her lips, she moaned and opened her mouth. He swept it and deepened the kiss, needing her to respond. Her tongue stroked his as her arms circled him and her hands explored his back. He was going to explode. But first he had to make sure she would burst into flame with him.

Shifting to his side, his hand settled on her waist. His thumb stroked up and down until she sidled closer, seeking more body contact. But if that happened, he'd be a goner.

Yet he didn't want to discourage her in any way. Sliding one of his hands between them, he teased her breast.

"Reed!"

"What?" he asked gently.

"You're…"

He palmed her breast and smoothed a finger around her nipple. "What am I doing?" he asked as he dropped a few kisses on her throat and pushed her hair back with his jaw, nibbling on her ear.

"You're…making me crazy."

He chuckled. "How about excited…aroused…"

"Those, too," she murmured.

Bending his head to her breast, his tongue rimmed her nipple and she quivered. When he did it again, her hands dipped to his buttocks to urge him toward her. He knew what she wanted but didn't know if she was ready. As he took her nipple into his mouth, she let out a small cry and her knee grazed him. He caught her leg and nudged it over his hip. Then he ran his hand up her thigh…stroking, caressing, making her more restless.

"Reed, what should I do?" she asked breathlessly.

"You're doing it," he rasped, sucking in a deep breath, restraining his desire until he was sure about hers.

Then he touched her.

Ten

From the moment Mallory had gazed into the mysterious, mesmerizing desire in Reed Fortune's eyes, she'd known she wanted him to make love to her. No man had ever made her feel so feminine or protected or excited, and the touch of his hands created a longing in her so deep it terrified her. His fingers had performed magic wherever they'd touched, and her body still trembled. Now as he caressed her thigh and found the center of her longing, tears came to her eyes. She wanted him there, inside her, and she wanted to give him everything she was.

But when she reached for him, he said in a hoarse murmur, "Wait a minute. I have to protect you."

The thought briefly passed through her mind that she didn't want to be protected from him, but before she could even open her eyes, he was back, rising above her, his heat becoming her heat, his desire hers.

"Trust me," he whispered right before he kissed her and took her arousal to an even higher pitch.

She wasn't sure what he meant. Thoughts swirled away into sensations as his tongue danced with hers, as his fingers touched her so intimately that she arched up to meet his hand, wanting something and needing it, not even sure what it was. When she felt him against her, she instinctively raised her hips to take him. He eased in with excruciating slowness, kissing her all the while. Then in a sparkling flash, he thrust into her and she felt a searing pain. But before it could completely register, he was moving slowly, erotically, causing sensations that had her gripping his shoulders and rocking against him. She became almost frantic with a need so powerful she knew she'd never want to feel it with anyone else. She knew she could never feel it *for* anyone else.

She loved Reed Fortune, and as her body strove to tell him how much, waves of sensation overtook her...pleasure so ecstatic she cried his name and dug her nails into his back. While she held on to him, he sank into her deeper and deeper and deeper until his release made him shudder again and again. His breathing was ragged, and as he finally took a deep breath and rolled to her side, she opened her eyes and looked at him.

They gazed at each other for long moments, slowly coming back to earth. Reed stroked her hair and tenderly caressed her cheek.

She was still lost in what had happened, thinking about how wonderful it had been, when she saw a change come over him.

His eyes no longer smiled at her, but became shuttered. His jaw became set. After he moved away from her a few inches and dropped his hand to his side, he cleared his throat.

She had a sense of foreboding that he was going to say something practical, something she didn't want to hear.

"Do you realize what we've done, Mallory? We're going to have to get a divorce now instead of an annulment."

The haze of happiness that had overtaken her during their lovemaking quickly cleared as reality hit her broadside. Reed was making it quite clear that this marriage was temporary. How could she have forgotten even for a second that he would be going back to Australia, that he was still probably in love with the woman he'd left there? Just because she loved him didn't mean he felt any more than desire for her.

Embarrassed now, feeling foolish because she'd mistaken passion for something else, she sat up and reached for the robe lying across the corner of the bed. Wrapping her pride around her as well as the robe, she responded, "We can always go to a tropical island somewhere and do it quickly." Her insides were still shaking, but she wouldn't let him see it. Just as she wouldn't let him see what he meant to her.

His eyes, filled with desire only a few minutes ago, now seemed remote. "That might be the most convenient. Once you're safely in Dawson's care." Sliding his legs over the side of the bed, he said, "I'm going to get a shower. Do you want to go out to dinner somewhere instead of cooking?"

What she wanted to do was to crawl into a corner and cry. She wasn't the least bit hungry, and the idea of sitting across a table from Reed and making small talk seemed impossible. But nothing was impossible, and she had to convince him that nothing had happened here that she couldn't forget, either. "Dinner sounds fine. Maybe a Tex-Mex place. I'm beginning to like the food here." She made her voice purposely cheerful.

"Tex-Mex, it is," he said gruffly, then went into the bathroom.

Mallory dropped her head into her hands as tears

welled up and threatened to overflow. But she took a few deep breaths and blinked them away. From now on, she would hide her feelings from Reed. She just prayed that Dawson would finish his out-of-town business more quickly than he planned.

Standing at the arrival gate at the San Antonio airport Saturday afternoon, Reed stared at each passenger who came off the plane, wishing Mallory had come with him, wishing Mallory would talk to him in other than the polite voice she'd used since he'd taken her to bed on Monday. They'd been strangers since. That afternoon, in that bed with her, had been more than pleasurable. Afterward, his world had felt changed and he'd been unnerved. She'd given him a gift and he'd accepted it, and then he realized he shouldn't have. San Antonio was a world away from Australia and he couldn't easily stay here, either legally or practically. His family depended on him. So he'd let Mallory put up a protective wall between them and he hadn't tried to break it down.

His gaze still on the gate, he saw his sister first, looking the way she always did—her thick, long blond hair in a braid, her blouse less than starched, her jeans worn and comfortable, and her gray eyes sparkling with their excitement for life. "Reed!" She came running toward him and threw her arms around him. "I missed you."

Laughing, he squeezed her hard, then leaned back. "Surprised by that, Matilda?" he teased.

"You bet." She glanced over her shoulder at Griff and Brody. "Maybe we can lock them up someplace while I'm here so I'll have a little fun."

"Define *fun*."

"We can start with you introducing me to some real Texas cowboys," she said.

"Over my dead body," Griff announced, coming up beside his sister.

"Over two very alive bodies," Brody added with a smile, and hugged Reed. "You look good, mate. Texas must agree with you."

Griff stood a little apart, watching as he always did. But he commented, "Or else it's his marriage."

Reed took a step away from Brody toward Griff, his quieter brother. "I'm glad you could come." He'd expected one of Griff's secret missions to take him away somewhere and he would have missed this chance to experience Texas and more family.

Griff just gave him a half smile that said he was glad to be here, too.

"So, where is this new bride?" Brody asked, looking around.

Reed had known his family would ask, and he was prepared. "She's working. Lily asked her to redecorate some rooms and they're meeting with a drapery designer this afternoon. She'll be at the ranch when we get there." At least he hoped she would, but maybe she'd try to avoid his family as well as him.

To change the subject, he asked them all, "How was Los Angeles?" They'd stopped there for a day to take a break from traveling so they wouldn't be exhausted when they reached San Antonio.

"The next time I pass through there," Matilda answered him, "I'm going to Disneyland."

He laughed. Matilda always made him laugh. She might be a little wild sometimes, but he liked having her around, and he *had* missed her. As they headed toward the baggage claim, Reed said, "Before I for-

get, Ryan and Lily are having a cocktail party tomorrow night in your honor. A lot of the family will
be there and some of their neighbors.''

''Uh-oh,'' Matilda said with a frown. ''Does that
mean I have to dress up?''

''It wouldn't hurt,'' Brody responded with some
amusement.

But as always, Griff came to his sister's rescue.
''Wear what you want, Matilda. I'm sure nobody will
care.''

As they drove to the Double Crown, Brody and
Matilda did most of the talking, filling Reed in on
everything that had happened at the Crown Peak
since he'd been gone. He went over some of the ob-
servations he had made about the operation at the
Double Crown, and the steps he'd like to take to
modernize when he got home, if they could convince
their father.

Brody and Matilda had just staunchly agreed to
back him up when he pulled up in front of Ryan and
Lily's house, relieved to see Mallory's sports car still
parked there.

''I like that car,'' Matilda said with a gleam in her
eye.

Reed just shook his head. ''I'll warn Mallory.''

At the door, he introduced the three of them to
Rosita, then they went into the great room where
Ryan, Lily, and Mallory were chatting. Ryan and Lily
stood and came forward, and greetings were exchanged all around. Then Mallory stepped into the
circle and Reed put his arm around her. It was the
first he'd touched her since— She seemed to freeze
under his arm. But she was smiling as she shook
Brody's hand, then Griff's and finally Matilda's. He

hoped his sister would watch her tongue. Sometimes she didn't. But she just smiled at Mallory, and it seemed as if the two women were sizing each other up. Mallory, too, wore jeans, though her white peasant blouse looked as if she'd just ironed it.

As Rosita brought them all cool drinks, they chatted for a while. Mallory became involved in a conversation with Matilda and Brody about the horses they raised. She was sitting next to Reed on the sofa, but her skin never brushed his and she focused her attention on his family.

Finally, Lily suggested, ''I know you're probably tired from traveling and would like to rest a bit. Why don't I show you to your rooms?''

''Oh, I don't want to rest,'' Matilda said. ''I want to see the horses.''

''I'll show you around,'' Mallory offered.

As Matilda looked at Reed, he just gave a shrug. ''Go ahead. I know you keep going from morning till night, and it won't be any different here.''

When Mallory stood, he clasped her arm. She looked at him, and he couldn't tell what she was thinking. ''I'll stay and spend some time with Griff and Brody. Lily's invited us to dinner.''

''I'll meet you back here in a little while then.''

He nodded, wishing he could establish a connection between them again...wishing for a lot more.

As Mallory walked to the barn with Matilda and told her what she'd been doing with the fillies and colts, she already liked Reed's sister. She was honest and expressive and said pretty much what was on her mind. After she had introduced Matilda to Hank and taken her through the mares' barn, they headed to the training arena.

Stepping inside, Matilda slipped her hands into her jeans' pockets. ''Reed hasn't told us very much about meeting you and the wedding. We're all trying to figure out why.''

''It happened so…fast,'' Mallory said cautiously.

''That's unlike Reed, too. He doesn't make an important decision without thinking about it first. Usually for a long time.''

''You'll have to ask him,'' Mallory responded.

Matilda gave her a speculative look.

The arena was empty for the time being. There wasn't much to see except for the building itself, but Matilda didn't seem to be in any hurry to leave. She walked toward the holding stalls to look them over. ''So…are there any cute, unmarried cowboys here you can introduce me to?''

Mallory had to think about it, then realized she couldn't answer Matilda. ''I don't know.''

Matilda smiled. ''You must really be in love with my brother if you're not noticing other men.'' Her gaze locked to Mallory's and held it.

''I suppose so,'' Mallory said quietly, admitting the truth again to herself, yet knowing she'd have to get over Reed. This week had been torture, trying to avoid him at every turn, making small talk, acting as if nothing had happened. She didn't know how much longer she could keep it up. At least with Reed's family here, they'd both have a distraction.

Matilda didn't ask any more personal questions as Mallory took her to the yearling pasture and through another barn, introducing her to Dusty Dawn and a few of the other horses. The whole time they chatted easily and then returned to the house. Dinner was enjoyable as they lingered over it, and conversation flowed. Griff had taken a seat next to Mallory, and she found him well-read and interesting to talk to. He drew her out about the trip to Europe she'd taken the summer after her freshman year at college, and she got the impression that he was well-traveled. It was almost eleven when she drove back to the cabin with Reed following her car in his truck. After they had gone inside, he asked, "What do you think of them?"

"They're very nice."

"You and Griff seemed to be hitting it off."

"He's a good listener."

"Yes, he is," Reed agreed. "But he listens well so he doesn't have to talk about himself."

When Mallory thought about it, she realized that Griff hadn't shared much personal information at all. "I forgot to tell you that Dawson called this morning. He's coming home Wednesday but then flying out again on Friday. Though he says he'll soon be back for good."

"I see. I suppose you're happy about that."

"Very happy," she said, lifting her chin, glad Reed wouldn't have to feel responsible for her for much longer.

They got ready for bed and didn't say much to each other after that. When she turned off her bedside lamp, she felt a deep sadness inside her, knowing it wasn't going to go away easily or anytime soon.

Observing the guests from her vantage point in the dining room at the hors d'oeuvre table the following evening, Mallory decided the cocktail party was a rousing success. Looking much younger than her twenty-one years in bib overalls and a white T-shirt, Matilda had moved from person to person, getting to know them, involved in animated conversation each time. More than once, Mallory had seen Griff standing apart simply watching everyone else as if he preferred it that way. For the moment she had lost track of Brody and Reed, but it was just as well. She had decided to dress up tonight, really dress. Her strapless violet sheath was an original. The V-bodice was trimmed in black, as was the hem, and her patent leather high heels felt a little strange after she'd been wearing boots and sneakers for so long.

But it was the look in Reed's eyes when he'd first seen her in the dress that had pleased her. He hadn't said anything, but the nerve in his jaw had twitched and he hadn't taken his eyes off of her for most of the night. She hadn't worn it to provoke him. She just needed to feel good about herself. It was the same reason she'd curled her hair and applied makeup. Maybe she just considered this her coming-out party.

A short while ago Lily had introduced her to two ranchers' wives and praised her talents as a decorator. One of them had said, "If you're going to be staying in the area, I'd certainly hire you."

The remark had given Mallory hope that she could succeed here.

Seeing that one of the cheese platters was almost empty, she picked it up to take it to the kitchen to refill. She'd seen Rosita pass through the dining room earlier on her way to the courtyard where more snack trays were located. But as Mallory entered the kitchen, she saw and heard Brody and Reed.

"I know it was fast," Reed was saying.

"Are you sure you didn't marry Mallory on the rebound?" Brody asked.

She stopped immediately, aware that she had interrupted a private discussion. But they knew she'd overheard and there was no getting around it.

"Will you give us a few minutes alone, Brody?" Reed asked his brother.

"This might take more than a few minutes," Brody responded as he glanced at Mallory apologetically and left the kitchen.

Mallory set the cheese dish on the counter and faced Reed. "Is that what Griff and Matilda think, too?"

"Anybody who sees you in that dress tonight should realize marrying you had nothing to do with being on the rebound."

He was talking about desire again, a man wanting a woman for purely physical reasons. She had hoped they'd gotten further than that. Yet hadn't the first time they'd made love proved her feelings were involved but his weren't? The hurt and sadness she'd felt this past week turned to anger. "You don't have to get married to have sex, Reed. I think it's about time you admit your motives for marrying me. You wanted revenge. You wanted to prove to your fiancée that you didn't need her. But in doing that you used *me* and you used me again when we...had sex."

His eyes were stormy blue and his voice vehemently deep. "Did *you* use *me?* Because there were two of us in that bed having an awfully good time."

A good time. A fling. An affair. Those were obviously what he wanted, and she didn't. There wasn't anything else to say.

His words still echoed as she tore her gaze from his and quickly went back into the dining room.

As Mallory passed through the great room, weaving in and out of the guests, she knew she had to be alone for a few minutes to compose herself. She headed for the powder room down one of the halls. But when she reached it, Matilda was there beside her. "Are you okay?"

She took a deep breath. "I'm fine."

"Brody told me he said something he shouldn't have, at least not with you within hearing distance. Did it cause a problem with you and Reed?"

She had a feeling Matilda wasn't going to let this go, and she might as well warn Reed's sister that this marriage wasn't going to be a marriage for very long.

"Reed and I have more than one problem."

With an appraising look, Matilda studied her. "And you don't want to talk about it."

"It's not that I don't want to, but there are reasons I shouldn't." Not that she believed Winston actually had any spies here, but their marriage had to appear real. Matilda was too honest to pretend it was if Mallory told her differently.

"Fair enough. But if you *do* need to talk, I can listen. I love Reed dearly, but, more than anybody, I know how frustrating he and the others can be."

Mallory had to smile at that. She'd always wanted a big brother, and she'd had Dawson on a limited basis. But she didn't know how she'd feel if she had three or more males trying to protect her and daily tell her what to do. "I'll remember that," she told Matilda, wishing they actually could be sisters-in-law, wishing she could truly be part of Reed's family.

But most of all, wishing Reed felt love in addition to desire.

On Monday afternoon, the salad that Mallory had made for lunch sat on the desk beside her as she estimated start-up costs for her shop. She'd realized she'd let her plans come to a standstill because of Winston and Clint Lockhart and Reed, so this morning she had done some real planning, budgeting, and written up a résumé.

She was about to take a bite of her salad when she heard the mail carrier's truck. He'd driven off by the time she'd walked outside to the mailbox at the end of the path. She recognized one envelope immediately. It had her stepfather's return address. She'd called her mother last week to reassure her she was fine. Yet she knew her mother didn't believe her.

Back in the cabin, Mallory laid the rest of the mail on the table and quickly opened his envelope. When she took out the letter, a check fluttered to the floor. Picking it up, she saw the amount and froze. Then she read the letter.

Dear Mallory,

I've accepted you as my daughter ever since I married your mother. We both know that marriage to Winston is the best course for you. We also realize that pride is holding you back from admitting you made a mistake when you ran off before the wedding. Therefore, we have found a way for you to keep your pride and still insure your future.

If this will end your charade of a marriage to Reed Fortune, you can cash this check, set up your own business and be an independent woman, as well as being married to Winston. In other words, you can have this portion of your inheritance now. I will have the bank release the funds to you as soon as you call me and tell me you are on your way home. We can handle an annulment or a divorce from here.

Don't let your pride stand in the way of your security and future happiness.

Sincerely,

George

Mallory didn't know whether to laugh, cry or scream. She was holding what most people would consider to be a fortune in her hand, and she didn't want it! Didn't George and her mother know her at all? Didn't they understand that she couldn't be bought? Going to the phone, she picked it up and dialed her stepfather's office number. She knew that he was the one behind this and that her mother went along with decisions he made. His secretary answered and put Mallory through immediately, as if she had been given orders to do so.

"Mallory, I'm so glad you called," George said in greeting. "I knew you would see the light."

"George, I can't accept this check. I *won't* accept this check."

"Now don't talk nonsense, Mallory."

"It's not nonsense. Being independent doesn't mean taking money from you. I intend to earn and pay my own way."

"But Winston says—"

"I don't care what Winston says. I am not marrying him, George, and that's final."

"This foolishness has got to stop, Mallory. Your mother is worried sick. She wants to see you settled with Winston—"

He wasn't listening again. He never listened. More than angry, she was just sad that he had such tunnel vision because it affected her mother, as well. "George, money will not bring me happiness. It can't buy me the things I want in life."

"You're a young woman who's never had to face reality. You have your head in the clouds if you think you can get through life on anything but a solid bank account. That check is a ticket to a marriage that will bring you social standing, a dowry that Winston will be glad to accept—"

"You want to bribe him to take me back?"

"Of course not. Winston doesn't need bribing."

"But I do?" She paused and regrouped. "George, now listen to me carefully. I'm going to keep your check, but I'm not going to cash it. I'm going to frame it. It's going to be my symbol of independence. Every time I look at it, I'll know what real independence is."

"You're a fool, Mallory."

"No. What I am is determined. You'll see."

Before he could give her another lecture, she hung up. She wouldn't be able to convince George or her mother of anything until she had proven herself. Well, that was exactly what she was going to do. Putting the check on top of the letter, she laid both safely inside the corner of the secretary, then sat there to go over her figures once more.

Eleven

Gray clouds swirled in the hazy white sky as Mallory drove to the barn later that afternoon. She wanted to ride. Her stepfather's check had created turmoil. Add to that what had happened with Reed last night at the cocktail party, and she couldn't sit still. If she could just slip into the barn and out again without anyone seeing her, she could go off on her own and sort through all of this.

The usual trucks and utility vehicles were parked near the barn. She saw Reed's among them. But fortunately only Hank was around when she went to Dusty Dawn's stall. She told him she was going to take the horse out for a ride.

Hank peered out at the sky. "Doesn't look like much is happening, but don't stay out too long. The storm's not going to be blowing over. I can feel it in my bones."

"I need some space around me, Hank."

Hank jerked his thumb outside. "Reed's over in the mares' barn consulting with the vet. Maybe you should talk to him first."

"I don't want to bother him. I'll be fine. Really."

"You could wait till Miss Matilda and Griff come back from Cruz's place...."

"It might be raining by then. I promise, if thunder rolls in, I'll come straight back."

The old cowhand still looked worried but helped her saddle up anyway. She rode out, not looking back, taking the route along the fence line where she had ridden with Reed.

As Mallory gave Dusty Dawn his head, she let the wind whip her hat to her back. It slapped against her, but she didn't care. She just wanted to run—from hurt, from anger, from Winston and her stepfather, from the visions of Reed making love to her, from her love for him. How could she feel so deeply in such a short amount of time?

Trees rushed by and Dusty's hooves kicked up dry earth behind them. She was so lost in her thoughts that the rumble of thunder barely registered. She just kept riding, not knowing where she was going, but knowing she didn't want to go back. Not yet. Then all of a sudden, lightning flashed over the horizon and Dusty's ears twitched.

She realized thunder definitely had rolled in. Patting his neck, she murmured, "It's okay, boy. We'll head back."

Looking around, she realized she'd ridden farther than she and Reed had, farther than she'd intended. She'd been so focused on running that she hadn't noticed where she was running to. As she brought Dusty to a lope, the scent of rain was strong in the wind. Finally she recognized the vee formation of a stand of live oaks on the crest of a hill, but by the time she turned south toward the Double Crown, the clouds opened and rain poured down as lightning flickered and thunder cracked.

"We're going to get wet, Dusty. No denying that."

She loosened her grip on the reins to snag her hat

and set it back on her head. But as she did, a jagged stab of lightning fired against the dark sky. Thunder boomed, and Dusty reared up, taking off on another run. Her balance jostled, Mallory's chin almost touched Dusty's mane as she grabbed for the reins.

Out of nowhere Reed came galloping toward her, and she groaned. She did *not* want to be rescued. Gathering her reins, she pulled them away from Reed as he grabbed for them at the same time.

"Why are you out here in this?" he yelled over the sound of the wind and rain.

"I needed to ride."

Even under the brim of his hat, she could see his eyes, and it was as if he noted the word "needed."

"You shouldn't be out here alone and you know it."

"No, I don't know it. Don't you understand? I needed some time alone."

The rain dripped from the brim of his hat. "Why must you always be so damned independent?"

He made "independent" sound like a terrible affliction. "Being independent is a good thing, not a character flaw."

With both of them now soaked to the skin, he shook his head. "Let's get going or Hank will be worried about us."

Sitting stiffly in the saddle, she nudged Dusty and took off ahead of Reed. But he soon caught up.

Hank was waiting for them back at the barn when they dismounted. "Looks like you two won't need no shower tonight." After giving the cowhand a weak smile, Mallory took Dusty's reins and led him into the barn. She heard Reed say, "We'll take care of the horses, Hank, if you want to quit for the day."

"I got a truck that needs some work over at the garage. I'll be there if anybody wants me."

Tossing her hat onto a bale of hay, Mallory took Dusty into his stall, unsaddled him, then rubbed him down. She imagined Reed was taking care of Spirit in a like manner, only when he was finished he'd turn the stallion into his pasture where there was a loafing shed if the horse didn't want to stand in the weather. The breeze whipping through the open barn door chilled Mallory. Her wet cotton blouse and jeans clung to her as she groomed Dusty, moving around him, wanting to take care of the horse before she took care of herself.

Just as she was closing the stall door, Reed came into the barn carrying a blanket. He thrust it at her. "Here, use this to dry off before you catch pneumonia."

His shirt and jeans were as wet as hers. Though his hair looked as if it had been kept fairly dry under his hat, hers was damp, the ends even wetter. She pushed the blanket back into his arms. "I don't need it, just as I didn't need you coming after me like some macho cowboy on a mission."

The vibrations emanating from him made every nerve of her body feel alive and tingling. She didn't want to feel it. She didn't want to look into his blue eyes and see his disapproval *or* his sense of responsibility. Grooming brush in hand, she headed for the tack room to put it away. But she had only gone about ten feet when he caught her in front of an empty stall. His hand on her shoulder clasped her firmly, but she didn't want to turn around. Yet she knew he wouldn't let go of her until she did.

She faced him squarely. "What do you want,

Reed? Do you want me to say thank you for watching over me? Thank you.''

''I don't want your thanks,'' he growled.

In the moment it took for her heart to beat, his lips crushed hers, and she knew exactly what he *did* want. Her wet blouse and his shirt met, practically giving off steam with the heat of their desire. If she considered pushing away, it was only for an instant before his tongue invaded her lips and she got lost again in the sensual pleasure of kissing him. He ravished her mouth until she melted against him, wanting him…needing him…loving him.

When he broke away, she stared up at him bereft, wondering if he was punishing her for keeping her distance, for denying the obvious desire between them.

His voice was gravelly as he said, ''I won't take what you don't want to give. Do you want this, too?''

''This'' to him was excitement and desire and arousal, but she did want it because she wanted *him*. She wanted his love, but maybe his desire would have to be enough. ''Yes, Reed,'' she responded to his question. ''I want this. I want you.''

''Mallory, you make me crazy,'' he said almost sternly, but then he took her face between his large hands and kissed her with the passion she could feel stringing his body…with a deep hungry need he'd called up inside of her from the moment they'd met.

When he dropped his hands, she almost protested until she felt him pull her blouse loose from her jeans. Taking his lead, she reached for the buttons of his shirt and unfastened them as quickly as she could, the wet material as well as his kiss distracting her. He had her blouse open before she managed his shirt.

Soon he'd unsnapped her jeans and was pushing them down her hips.

This time *she* broke the kiss. "You're too far ahead."

He laughed, then pulled off his boots and took her with him down onto the fresh straw inside the stall. It was prickly but she hardly noticed as he ridded her of her boots and jeans and panties. Her fingers fumbled with the leather of his belt and when her hand brushed his fly, he groaned. She grated the zipper down, knowing they were both past teasing, whispers and foreplay. She shrugged out of her blouse as he shed his shirt, then they stared at each other for a moment. The intense look in his eyes told her he was waiting for her to say stop...waiting for her to run away. But she couldn't. She wanted so much from Reed that if she had to settle for this heated coming together, she would.

She knew he was waiting for a signal from her and when she glanced at his arousal, she could almost feel it pulsing with the beat of her heart. "I only have one piece left," she murmured, referring to her lacy bra.

"I know," he said in a tight voice.

"Do you want to take it off, or should I?" she asked.

A dark flush swept his cheekbones as he came to his knees and reached around her. The lace fell away. Holding her at her waist, he brought his lips to one nipple. She laced her hand in his hair and moaned at the sensual, erotic rasp of his tongue as he teased the bud over and over. The apex of her thighs throbbed. She was hot, and she needed him in the most primitive way a woman could need a man.

His hands, the calluses sensually arousing, came up her sides, and as he raised his head, he covered her breasts with his palms. "I've dreamed of doing this again." His deep tone was rich with desire.

"What else?" she encouraged him.

"Everything," he muttered, then kissed her, a deep possessive kiss. Bringing her down with him, he pulled her on top of him. Instinctively knowing what he wanted, she straddled his hips, then slowly—oh, so slowly—sank down onto him.

She trembled from the wonder of receiving him, taking him, pleasuring him. His shudder as he thrust up into her told her he was near the edge. Yet she should have known he wouldn't search for his own satisfaction without taking her along.

"Come here," he said hoarsely as he raised his hands.

She leaned into them, and he stroked her breasts, arching into her at the same time, creating a fiery escalating excitement that was making her breathless. Then one of his hands slipped between their bodies, and she thought she'd burst from the glorious sensation. He thrust again, touching her at the same time until the arousing ripple built and built and built, finally exploding in a shattering burst of pleasure. Her body was still loving his when his climax hit and his groans reverberated through her. In this moment, they were one, and she needed to hold on to him for as long as she could.

When his breathing slowed, she raised herself up and gazed into his eyes. He didn't say anything or move anything and she wondered if she had done something wrong…if maybe she'd been too wanton. Beginning to feel embarrassed, she started to shift away from him, but he settled his hands on her hips and ordered, "Don't move. I just want to look at you."

She could feel a blush sweeping over her. "I'm sure I look a mess." Her fingers went to her damp hair.

But his gaze didn't waver and his hands stayed firmly in place. "You're beautiful, Mallory. You could never look a mess if you tried."

Her eyes pricked with tears. "Thank you."

A smile crept across his lips. "And you can even be a lady at a time like this."

She knew he was teasing her and she smiled. The straw was prickling her knees and she said to him, "You've got to be terribly uncomfortable."

This time he gave her a full-fledged grin. "Not as uncomfortable as I was about fifteen minutes ago."

"Are you trying to embarrass me to death?"

He shook his head, and then his expression became serious. "Mallory, we didn't use protection. I want you to know—"

"Let's just take one day at a time," she suggested. "I'm having enough trouble with that." She didn't want him offering her money. The idea of having Reed's baby was a wonderful thought. When he did go back to Australia and leave her, if she was pregnant, she'd have someone special to love, someone to remind her of him.

She did move away from him now, but he opened his arms to her. "Come here."

When she lay beside him, he held her close and kissed her temple. "It won't hurt to take a few minutes to catch our breath."

Lying here beside him this way, normal breathing

was impossible. She heard a horse snort, a tail swish. The smell of hay and rain and earth was all around her, but so was the scent of Reed, and she loved breathing him in. "What if someone comes in?"

"We're married, remember? This isn't against the law."

Married. How she wished that were really true. But no amount of wishing could keep Reed here or make him love her. As she'd told him, they'd just have to take one day at a time.

After they dressed, laughing about their still-wet clothes, they drove back to the cabin. Reed parked first, then came to her car and opened her door for her. The rain had stopped and the sky was brightening. They walked to the door, comfortable, their arms brushing.

Reed said, "Ryan has a whole slew of tickets for a rodeo Wednesday night. He thought we'd all enjoy it. Do you want to go?"

"That sounds like fun. Only...Dawson should be getting in Wednesday afternoon."

"There's a ticket for him, too." Reed smiled at her.

"Fortunes will probably take up the whole grandstand," she teased.

"Probably."

Once in the cabin, Reed went to the bedroom for some dry clothes, wondering how to ask Mallory if they'd be sleeping in the bed together that night. It was all he could think of—holding her in his arms all night. But before he could figure out the best way to put it into words, the telephone rang. When Mallory said, "I'll get it," he opened a drawer and took out a pair of jeans. But a moment later she was standing in the bedroom doorway, her expression odd. "It's for you. Stephanie Milton."

What could Stephanie possibly want and why had she chosen this moment to call? Since he couldn't answer either of those questions, he went to the phone and picked up the receiver that Mallory had laid on the counter. "Hello? Stephanie?"

"Reed? Hello. How are you?"

He didn't know if Mallory was listening or not, but he wouldn't blame her if she was. "I'm fine."

"You probably want to know why I'm calling when I... I just wanted to see how you were. I'm sorry for writing you a letter like that, but I didn't know what else to do."

"You could have told me what was going on. You could have called. You could have asked me to come home."

There was a short silence. "But I didn't do any of those things for a reason."

He'd always had to pull everything out of her. She was so unlike Mallory who wasn't afraid to speak her mind. "What reason?" he asked.

"You're so strong-willed, Reed. I was afraid I couldn't stand up to you. Sometimes I...I just can't tell you what I want to tell you. This way I could. I met Jack before you left, and I didn't want to admit how I felt. He knew right away we were right for each other, and I guess I did, too. But I was afraid to rock the boat, and I didn't want to have to tell you or your family. But your going away seemed to be a blessing. He's right for me, Reed. I belong with him."

He could make his ego feel better and tell her he'd

gotten married—apparently she hadn't contacted his parents and didn't know. Yet what purpose would that serve, especially when he'd be divorced before he went back? The thought of that divorce made him feel a lot worse than Stephanie's letter had. There was some analyzing he had to do here, but he wasn't going to use Stephanie to do it or make her feel bad in the process.

"Thank you for calling, Stephanie. But I'm fine. You did what you had to do. I wish you and your husband much happiness."

After another minute or so of good wishes and goodbyes, he hung up the receiver. With what Stephanie had said playing through his mind, he stopped in the doorway to the bedroom. Mallory had laid out a change of clothes for herself.

She looked up at him, her expression serious, her eyes asking him questions he didn't know the answers to. In the expectant silence, he knew she was waiting for him to explain the call, to acknowledge what had happened between them, to let her know what happened next. But a lot of it depended on her.

"Stephanie just wanted to check in and make sure I was okay."

The silence between them grew long until Mallory asked, "Do you still have feelings for her?"

Yes, he still cared about Stephanie, but... "We knew each other for a long time, Mallory. We were friends before we got engaged."

"I see," Mallory responded, and he wondered exactly what she saw.

When she didn't say anything else, he knew he had to get to the heart of their relationship by asking,

"Are we going to be sleeping in the same bed tonight?"

She looked startled for a moment, then her eyes flashed with the same indignation he heard in her voice. "I don't think that would be a good idea. In fact, on Wednesday I'll try to pin Dawson down on an exact date when he's going to be back and I can move into his apartment. That would be best for both of us."

When she went into the bathroom and shut the door with a click, he swore, knowing there was nothing he could do about Mallory leaving, knowing what had happened in the barn wasn't about to happen again anytime soon.

The smell of horses and leather and raring-to-go excitement rode heavy on the evening air as Reed walked with Dawson outside the bull pens. Mallory, along with Gwen and Zane, Dallas and Maggie, Cruz and Savannah, sat up in the stands near the roping gates, waiting for the rodeo to begin. When Dawson had asked Reed if he wanted to go look at the bulls, he'd nodded. Mallory was staying as far away from him as possible. She'd told Dawson she would save seats for everyone from the Double Crown who hadn't yet arrived.

Reed stopped to study one of the bulls who would either win some cowboy a purse or throw him to the dust.

Coming up beside him, Dawson said, "Mallory seems quiet tonight."

It was an opening, but Reed didn't know if he wanted to take it. "She gets quiet sometimes."

"You know," Dawson began casually, "it's amazing how much I learned about her through the letters she wrote and our phone calls now and then. Tonight I think she's more than quiet.''

Reed glanced at Dawson. He was wearing jeans tonight and boots and a Western-cut shirt, but he still looked more like a chief financial officer than a cowboy. He was the only one who knew the whole truth about their marriage and maybe he could help Reed figure out Mallory. ''I got a phone call yesterday from my former fiancée.''

Dawson leaned a hip against the bull pen's rough wood. ''I see.''

''What do you see?'' Reed asked. ''Stephanie's married now. End of story.''

A gate clanged and a trio of cowboys strode by before Dawson said, ''Mallory probably doesn't figure it quite that way. Are you sure this marriage of yours is simply one of convenience?''

Thinking about yesterday in the barn, Reed wasn't sure about anything. There was no way he was going to tell Dawson he'd taken his sister to bed. ''I'm just making certain she's kept safe until you can do the job. I've got a life back in Australia, and she's told me over and over again she wants to put down roots here, independent of a man who might try and tell her what to do or force her into something she doesn't want.''

''That all might be true, but it doesn't mean that she can't be jealous.''

''Mallory? Jealous? Of Stephanie? She doesn't even know the woman.''

''But she probably has a vision of her in her mind. I know you say this is just a marriage of convenience, but if it weren't, she might think you're comparing her to this woman you were engaged to.''

Could Mallory think he was comparing her to Stephanie? Is that what this was all about?

They started back to the stands and had passed the entrance gate when Reed glanced at the bleachers and saw Ryan and Lily making their way up the steps. Then he spotted Brody and Matilda buying sodas from one of the concession stands. The smells of popcorn and French fries mixed with the scent of hay and animals.

Bumping Dawson's elbow, he said, ''Come over here. There's somebody I want you to meet.'' Matilda was just stuffing change into her pocket when he came up behind her.

''Howdy, cowgirl. Ready to ride those saddle broncs?'' Reed asked his sister with a grin.

Swinging around quickly, she smiled at him. ''As ready as you are.''

''Matilda, this is Dawson Prescott. Dawson, meet my sister, Matilda Fortune.''

Dawson looked a bit startled as his eyes seemed glued to Matilda and passed over her tousled braided hair, over her wrinkled T-shirt and jeans, to the tips of her dusty boots. ''I thought your sister was older,'' he commented to Reed.

Reed wondered about the sparks in Dawson's eyes as he kept looking at Matilda.

''Just how old do you think I am?'' Matilda asked Dawson, a slight snap to her tone.

''Eighteen?'' he guessed.

''Try twenty-one,'' she said with a smug smile. ''Now maybe I should guess *your* age.''

Dawson didn't look any too happy to have been challenged but shrugged gamely. "Go ahead."

Her gaze swept over him as his had swept over her. "Thirty-three."

"Thirty-two," he corrected with a frown.

"Guess I'm a better judge of age than you are, even though I *am* young."

Reed knew his sister, and her back was up. Before this got ugly, he knew he'd better step in. "Dawson is Mallory's half brother."

Soda in hand, Brody came to join them, and Reed introduced the two men.

Dawson shook Brody's hand. "I'll be spending the day with you tomorrow, helping you familiarize yourself with the files and any other information you might need at the offices."

"Reed told me you're head honcho of finances over at Fortune. I'm looking forward to getting started."

"I have to fly out again on Friday, but in about a week, I'll be back to stay for a while," Dawson explained.

"It will probably take me that long to get acquainted with everything."

Brody had just told Reed that Griff had stayed back at the Double Crown when music suddenly blared from the loudspeakers and a horseman rode into the middle of the ring carrying an American flag. Reed pointed to the section of bleachers where the Fortunes were seated. As the group walked toward them, Reed heard Matilda say to Brody, "I'm glad you're the one who will be working with Prescott. Stuffed shirt, if you ask me."

Reed just shook his head. One of these days when

Matilda spoke her mind, she was going to get into trouble.

The national anthem began playing and everyone in the stands stood. Reed took his place next to Mallory, but she stared straight ahead.

Annoyed with her standoffishness, he purposely let his shoulder brush hers.

She glanced at him, then fixed her gaze on the center of the rodeo ring once more. After the anthem finished playing and they sat on the bleachers, Mallory said, "Dawson told me he would be home for good by the end of next week. So I'll be moving out. I can leave the rugs and things, if you'd like, except for the desk. I'm going to need that."

The thought of Mallory moving out made Reed's gut clench, but he wasn't about to let her see that. "You can take it all with you."

When she didn't glance at him again, he told himself what they had was an *inconvenient* marriage that would be ending very soon.

Twelve

At almost 11:00 p.m. Reed turned onto the road leading to the Double Crown. Dawson and Mallory were carrying on a conversation about the rodeo circuit. Reed's mood was sober as he considered the fact that Mallory was going to move out. It *was* a fact. Add to that his telephone conversation with Stephanie, and he examined all of it very carefully.

Stephanie's words had bothered him. *You're so strong-willed, Reed. I was afraid I couldn't stand up to you.*

Why hadn't he seen the problem? Why hadn't he realized Stephanie's quietness was more than shyness? Why hadn't he given her a chance to express herself?

But then he thought about Mallory, her spirit, the way she confronted him. He'd all but forgotten Stephanie since he'd met Mallory. What did that say about his feelings for his former fiancée? Had he decided to marry her simply because it was time to settle down and she'd been acceptable and convenient?

Hard questions he had to answer if he wanted any peace.

When he pulled onto the gravel driveway at the adobe, he didn't cut the engine. Glancing over his shoulder at Dawson, who was sitting in the back seat, he asked, "Are you staying for a while?"

"Don't you usually get up early in the morning?" Dawson asked.

"I'd like to go up to the barn and check on a mare who cut her leg, but I don't like to leave Mallory here alone after dark."

"No problem," Dawson agreed.

"I don't need a baby-sitter," Mallory murmured. "Dawson, we have a security system now. If you want to leave—"

"I'll just come in for something to drink. You can show me the budget you told me about for your shop."

Reed frowned. Mallory hadn't told him about her budget. But then, she hadn't been talking to him about much of anything.

After Dawson had followed Mallory into the cabin, Reed backed out of the driveway and drove to the barn and parked. He thought he heard the sound of another car, but when he climbed out of the truck, the night was silent. A floodlight illuminated the front of the barn. Reed knew one of the security guards Ryan had hired checked the premises about every half hour, but there was no sign of anyone else now.

He was opening the horse's stall when he heard footsteps behind him. Before he could turn around, three men jumped him. All of them wore ski masks. The burliest bloke, as tall as Reed was, caught him in a choke hold, while a second delivered a blow to his ribs. The rest was a blur as Reed landed a right to a jaw and shoved his elbow into one of his attacker's midsections. But there were three of them, and one of him. They knew exactly where to land blows for the best effect—his jaw, the back of his neck, his solar plexus.

One of them leaned over him and said clearly and succinctly, "Send Mallory Prescott back to San Francisco or the next time will be even more fun."

Then they were gone, leaving him bleeding on the damp cement.

"Are you sure you want to move out?" Dawson asked Mallory after he took a long swallow of iced tea.

"This arrangement was only temporary," Mallory answered. They'd kept the conversation casual all evening, but she knew it was headed in another direction now as they sat on the sofa. With a sideways glance at him, she added, "With Lily's commission and my savings, I should be able to get my own apartment if you don't want me to move in with you. I know I just turned up on your doorstep, so to speak, and I don't want to disrupt your life."

"You won't be disrupting my life," he said quickly. "I'll be glad to have you. But watching you and Reed together, I wonder how easy it will be for you to leave."

Could Dawson sense the hum of sexual energy between her and Reed? Or was her love for her husband that obvious? "It won't be easy, but it's necessary." Setting her glass on the coffee table, she shifted toward him. "I think you should tell me more about *your* life."

"My life is my work and coming out here on weekends to relax. That's about it."

"No one special?" she asked gently.

He shook his head, and when she looked into his eyes, she saw a protective shield there. "Why not?"

"Too high-risk."

"You can't put loving someone in the same category as an investment," she responded, though her own heart hurt because she knew exactly what Dawson meant.

"I saw what my mother went through when our father left her to marry your mother. The bitterness and resentment still color her world. I don't ever want to do that to someone, or have them do it to me."

"Dawson..."

"I mean it, Mallory. It's non-negotiable."

"But don't you get...lonely?" she asked, thinking that when she'd made love with Reed, when they'd talked and teased and just spent time together, her heart and soul were satisfied in a way they never had been before.

"I'm too busy to be lonely."

She knew better than that, and she'd sensed something tonight—a change in Dawson after Matilda had arrived. He'd glanced at Reed's sister quite often as they'd sat on the bleachers. "What do you think of Reed's sister?"

"She's young."

"She's twenty-one!"

"She's fresh off the ranch with more sass than experience, and from what I understand from Reed, she was a hellion growing up."

Before Mallory could process his vehemence about Matilda—something that sounded more like interest than dismissal—the phone rang. Looking at her watch, she saw it was almost midnight. Maybe Reed had gotten tied up with the horse.

But when she answered the phone, it was a male voice other than Reed's. "Mallory, it's Griff. Something's happened."

There was a note in his tone that made her heart start hammering. "Is it Reed?"

"Three men jumped him in the barn."

Her breath caught. "Is he all right?"

Griff hesitated. "They knew what they were doing, Mallory. He's going to be pretty sore and stiff, but I don't think it's serious. Against Reed's protests, Ryan called a friend who's a doctor. He just arrived." After a pause Griff went on. "Reed talked to Ryan about the men, but he won't say anything to us. He says he has to talk to you first."

"I'll be right there." Tears came to her eyes when she thought about Reed being hurt.... Did this have something to do with Winston? Or with Clint Lockhart? She brushed the tears away. She had to make sure that Reed was truly all right...and then, if this was Winston's doing, she had to think about leaving.

When Mallory arrived at Ryan's, the doctor was in one of the guest rooms examining Reed. She wanted to rush into the room, but she knew she should wait until the doctor was finished. Lily and Matilda stayed by her side, saying supportive things, but she could tell they were as worried as she was.

Brody came over to her. "I didn't mean to insult you or cause trouble between you and Reed the other night at the party."

"I know you didn't. You care about Reed. That's what brothers are for."

Tilting his head, Brody said, "I think you're good for him. For what it's worth."

"It's worth a lot," she said softly.

When Reed's brother put his arm around her shoulders and gave her a squeeze, tears came to her eyes.

Finally the doctor emerged from the bedroom, leaving the door ajar. "He thinks he's Crocodile Dundee," the elderly man said with a shake of his head. "But nothing's broken, no signs of concussion. Internal organs sound and feel fine. His ribs are sore, and he has bruises—those will look worse before they look better. But other than that, he should be okay. Tie him down tonight if you have to, so he gets some rest. He really should stay in bed tomorrow, too, but I doubt if he will." The doctor shook his head again. "One tough Australian."

"Can I go in?" Mallory asked.

"If he doesn't come out first," the doctor joked.

With a feeling of relief bringing tears to her eyes again, she stepped inside the room.

Reed was sitting on the edge of the bed, his soft chambray shirt open down the front, his hands braced on the side of the mattress. His lip was split, and there was a long, red, purplish discoloration along his jawline. He seemed oblivious to her, and she wondered exactly how much pain he was in. She wanted to start crying all over again. But that was silly, and it wouldn't help him.

"Reed?" she asked softly.

He raised his head then, and she could see his chest had the same red mark as his jaw.

"What can I do?" she asked.

"Pack me in ice." His almost-smile was crooked.

Going closer, she knelt in front of him. "Do you

have any idea who did this? Everyone's suggesting it had something to do with Clint Lockhart—"

"This is Bentley's fault."

"How do you know?"

"Because one of them gave me a message. I'm supposed to send you back to California, or the next time will be worse."

"Oh, Reed. Maybe I should go back and have this out with Winston."

"You're not going anywhere near him. If they did this to me, God knows what they'd do to you."

"But you'll be in danger if I stay."

He closed his eyes for a moment. "Can we talk about this after I get some ice? I want to go back to the cabin."

"Do you think you should? Move around, I mean?"

"If I don't move around, I'm not going to be able to move. Let's go." When he stood, she wasn't sure he was steady. But as she slipped her arm around him, he jerked away. "I'm fine, Mallory."

Why couldn't he need her, just a little bit?

Out in the hall, he brushed away everyone's concern. "I just need a good night's sleep."

"I'll drive you," Dawson said.

When Reed looked as though he might try to macho his way through driving back, too, Mallory intervened. "Please let Dawson drive."

"All right," he mumbled grudgingly.

Ryan handed him his hat. "If you need anything, you call me."

Reed nodded and made his way down the hall. He walked through the great room slowly, but under his own steam. In the foyer, Matilda gave him a careful hug; Brody clasped his shoulder. But Griff said, just loud enough for Mallory to overhear, "If you need to do anything about this, I'll help you."

The thought of the two brothers taking on Winston Bentley made her very nervous—and worried.

At the adobe, Mallory hopped out of the back seat of Dawson's luxury sedan and opened the front door for Reed. He glanced up at her, but she knew he wouldn't accept her help. He'd get out of the car on his own steam, no matter how much it hurt. Once inside the cabin, he started for the sofa, but she said, "Take the bed, Reed, please."

He gave her a long look, then went to the bed and stretched out.

Dawson was standing at the door. "I think I'm going to leave you two alone. He doesn't want anybody to see him like this. But you call me if there's any problem, and I'll stop over tomorrow to check on him."

"Thank you, Dawson." Her voice got husky.

He wrapped her in a big hug. "It's going to be okay, Mallory."

She closed the door behind Dawson and made sure the security alarm was activated.

Lily had given her three ice bags that they kept on hand. After putting two of them in the freezer, Mallory wrapped one in a fresh towel and took it into Reed. His eyes were closed, his shirt wide open. The marks and scrapes on him were becoming more obvious. But even in his beat-up condition, she found him to be the sexiest man alive.

Opening his eyes, he trained them on her. "I'm not sure where to put the ice first."

"I have more than one pack. How about some acetaminophen? That might help a little."

"I'll get it." He tried to prop himself up on his elbows and turn so he could slide out of bed without hurting his ribs.

Giving his shoulder a gentle shove, she ordered, "Stay put." When her thumb met his shirt, she couldn't turn away from his mesmerizing blue eyes.

He cleared his throat. "I have to move to the sofa, anyway."

"No. You stay right there. You should probably get your clothes off so you're more comfortable."

"Wanna help me?" he asked with a glimmer of amusement in his eyes.

Reed getting hurt had taught her something about loving him. She'd rather love him while she could, rather than push away from him. "You're not in any condition for what you're suggesting."

"And if I was?" His expression had gone dead serious.

"I'd help you take your clothes off," she answered in almost a whisper.

He didn't comment on her change of course but pulled a long breath of air into his lungs. "Well, then, maybe you should get comfortable, too, and come hold the ice bag for me."

It was an invitation she wasn't going to refuse. She couldn't wait to curl up next to him…tend to him, love him, any way she could, for as long as she could. "I'll get your pills and be right back." She laid the ice bag on the bed and went into the bathroom.

When she emerged with a small cup of water and the pills, he'd managed to undress down to his briefs,

but the effort had cost him. Sweat beaded his brow.
He was seated on the edge of the bed again as if he
had to shore up his strength before he could stretch
out.

Fetching a pillow from behind the sofa bed, she
laid it on top of the one already there so he'd be more
comfortable. Then he swung his legs up and lay back
with a wince. "I guess we'd better put that ice on
the ribs."

Quickly undressing, she pulled on her nightgown,
then lay next to him, settling the ice bag across his
ribs. "Can I get you anything else?"

"You could kiss it all away," he said, half joking,
half serious.

Mallory, oh, so carefully, gently kissed his bruised
jaw and then his split lip.

His arm came around her. "Mallory..." His voice
was filled with the same need she saw in his eyes.
But she knew he needed rest more than he needed
anything else. She pushed his hair back from his
brow as she'd wanted to do so very often. "You need
to sleep now, Reed. I'll be right here. I'm not going
anywhere."

"Stay close," he murmured as he closed his eyes.

She curled up beside him, careful not to hurt him,
knowing she had lost her heart irrevocably.

The sun wasn't quite up when she felt Reed move.
"Do you need another ice bag?" she asked.

"I need you."

The way he was looking at her in the predawn
light, she knew he meant it. "You shouldn't."

"That doesn't mean I can't."

Her gaze dropped to his briefs where it was very

evident what he could do. ''Maybe you should put the ice bag down there,'' she teased.

''You're a little witch,'' he responded, slipping his hand under her hair, cradling her head, bringing her to him. ''Kissing's a little tough right now,'' he murmured as his lips brushed her cheek and then over her mouth.

''I think everything else would be, too.''

''The pleasure would definitely be worth the pain,'' he whispered into her ear. His beard stubble was an erotic tease against her skin, his breath warm and sensual.

''Are you sure?''

''Positive,'' he answered. But when he went to prop himself up on his elbow, he couldn't, and he swore.

She wanted to give him a gift for everything he'd given her. But she didn't know if he'd accept it. Kissing his forehead, she murmured, ''It's all right. Stay still. We'll do this another way.'' Before he could protest, she slipped her nightgown over her head and lay naked beside him.

He managed to skim off his briefs and drop them to the floor. ''You can straddle me,'' he said, his voice husky.

''I'm afraid I'll hurt you. Let me just try something else.'' Before he had a chance to ask her what, her hand tenderly slid over his navel. When he sucked in a breath, she knew it was pleasure, not pain. He was fully aroused. Bending to him, her hair brushed his stomach, and then she touched her lips to him.

''Mallory, you can't.''

She raised her head. ''Oh, yes, I can. Let me do

this for you, Reed. Please. You've done so much for me.''

It was several moments until he gave her an almost imperceptible nod. She bent toward him again and loved him with her hands, and her lips and her tongue—soft caresses, gentle sucking, long strokes—until he clasped her shoulder and roughly said, ''Turn onto your side.'' Somehow he managed to roll onto his. Then he took her leg over his hip and eased into her.

Arousing him had aroused her, and she met each thrust, wanting to give him as much pleasure as he could handle. But he was giving her pleasure, too. He caressed her thigh, then touched the flash point of her pleasure until an undulating wave of ecstasy rolled over her, lifting her, throwing her, sweeping her closer to him. Her name was a deep guttural groan as he found his own release and clasped her to him tightly.

When they opened their eyes, they gazed at each other. ''You're a special woman, Mallory.''

She wanted to tell him he was more than special to her, that he was the love of her life...her only love...her true love. But she couldn't go chasing off after him to Australia when her life had to be sorted out here. Besides, he'd made no mention of his feelings, and for all she knew, they were still wrapped up in Stephanie Milton.

Mallory and Reed were still joined when she said, ''I should leave. I don't want to put you in any more danger. I should have known when I overheard Winston—'' She stopped.

''What did you overhear?''

She told Reed about the conversation she'd over-heard before she'd left San Francisco.

After listening, Reed muttered, "We're going to get him off of our backs, once and for all."

"But how can we?"

He kissed her forehead. "I'm going to shower, then call Dawson and Griff. After a strategy session, I'll tell you how."

Reed's jaw had turned more black and blue, but the determined set of it told her she couldn't dissuade him from whatever plan he was coming up with. After he showered, he made the two phone calls. He was moving slowly, but moving, and she realized that nothing was going to keep him down. But she had her own plans on how she was going to get him to rest for the day.

When he hung up the phone, he explained, "Dawson's going to call me after he gets what I need."

"What do you need?"

"Dirt on Bentley. Dawson says Sam Waterman isn't only a security expert, but he knows some of the best P.I.'s in the business. We should have something by this afternoon. Griff's going to meet us here around five. The only way to get Bentley is to beat him at his own game, and I can do that if I have the right information."

Stepping close to him, she said, "I don't want you to get hurt again."

He enfolded her in his arms. "I don't intend to."

She was naked, too, and their heartbeats synchro-nized. Tipping her head up, she offered, "I could bring you breakfast in bed."

"Is this a bribe so I'll stay here today?"

"Could be. Will it work?"

"Only if you'll let me do for you what you did for me early this morning."

The pictures that exploded in her head excited her and aroused her just thinking about them. "I'll let you do anything you want," she promised, standing on tiptoe to kiss him, hoping she could make him forget about Stephanie Milton altogether.

When Reed received the information he needed, realizing he should have gone on the offensive earlier with Bentley, he developed a plan. According to Sam Waterman, most of Bentley's deals were a matter of public record, and he trod a thin legal line. But what went on behind the scenes wasn't on the public record, and that's where Reed needed to concentrate. As he discovered, using the information Dawson had secured for him, Bentley usually bought whatever he wanted. When he couldn't, he terrorized until he got it.

Monday morning, five days after Bentley's men had jumped him, Reed and Griff flew to San Francisco—against Mallory's protests. Reed had decided not to take the company jet; he didn't want to announce to Bentley that he was coming. The worry in Mallory's eyes had bothered him, but he knew this was something he had to do to get her free of Bentley. When he wasn't on the phone investigating further leads over the weekend, they'd spent the rest of the time in bed. The desire he felt for her was all-consuming and never seemed to lessen. He didn't understand it now, any more than he had the first night he'd met her.

When he and Griff arrived in San Francisco, they checked into a hotel and then visited one person after another—all people Bentley had stepped on—and documented everything they could. None of Bentley's victims could be convinced to file charges or testify against him. Some of them had been hurt physically by Bentley's thugs, but insisted they didn't want to cause trouble because they had families to protect. Yet Reed suspected they could be prodded if they knew they weren't alone. But it would take reassurance...convincing...and time. He needed to insure Mallory's safety *now*.

Reed had reserved an executive suite. That night after phoning Mallory, who was staying at the big house for safety's sake, and exchanging erotic words with her about what they'd do when he got home, he typed up a lengthy report and printed several copies.

Griff, who had insisted on coming with him, was a valuable asset, knowing exactly what questions to ask. But on Tuesday morning, Reed went to Winston Bentley IV's office alone.

The building was steel and smoked glass, and Bentley's suite of offices was luxuriously appointed. Reed stood in front of the man's secretary. "I want to see Winston Bentley."

"Do you have an appointment?" she asked.

"No. Just tell him Reed Fortune is here. He'll see me."

She looked curiously at Reed's bruised jaw, and then pressed the intercom and announced him. A few moments later she said, "You can go back. Second door on the right."

Knowing he had to challenge Bentley on his own turf, he strode down the hall. The door to the office was open, and he stepped inside.

Bentley didn't bother to stand. "I hope this is important. I have an appointment in fifteen minutes."

There was no point wasting time in verbal battle. Reed slapped a manila envelope onto Bentley's desk. "It shouldn't take you that long to read this."

Bentley's eyes darted to the envelope. "Why would I want to do that?"

"Because if you or anyone you employ ever comes near Mallory or me again, I'll make sure that these people band together against you."

Picking up the envelope, Bentley pulled out the report inside and scanned it. "These people will never testify against me," he responded smugly.

"Maybe...maybe not. But if you lift a finger to hurt Mallory or me again, I won't wait for them to band together. I'll go to the press and expose you for the terrorist and swindler you are."

"Look here, Fortune. Mallory doesn't need your interference or anything else you can provide. With her stepfather's inheritance..." He stopped as if waiting for a reaction.

Reed didn't know what Bentley was getting at and he didn't care. "This isn't open for discussion. Stay away from her or you'll be sorry."

Without waiting for a response, he turned and left Winston Bentley IV's office.

Remembering the look of chagrin that had passed over Bentley's face briefly when he'd seen the report, Reed took the elevator down to the lobby. When he exited it, he saw Griff standing by a potted palm, arms folded over his chest. Sometimes his brothers were as frustrating as they were loyal. As he reached

Griff, he said, "I thought I told you I wanted to do this alone."

Griff said simply, "You did."

With a wry grin, Reed hung his arm around his brother's shoulders. "Let's go back to San Antonio."

Thirteen

To keep from worrying about Reed, Mallory had kept busy since he'd left. Their weekend together had been so wonderful that, when he'd left for California, she'd missed him desperately. She couldn't imagine how she'd feel when he went back to Australia, and there was no doubt that he would.

Ryan had insisted Mallory stay with them up at the house, rather than at the adobe, and she hadn't argued. She felt part of their family now, and spent many of her hours with Matilda. She was watching Reed's sister work a two-year-old filly in the corral when Hank yelled for Mallory, and she saw a Federal Express truck parked by the barn. Crossing to the gate, she opened it and met the driver there. He asked for her signature, and she signed for an overnight letter. It was from Winston.

Tempted to toss it without opening it, she decided it was better to know her enemy than to ignore him. Inside she found a copy of a real estate contract, a brochure with a picture of a magnificent house and a letter from Winston.

Mallory—
This will be our home. Note the pool out back. I told the real estate agent that your name will

go on the title with mine. Just sign the enclosed contract and mail it back to her. If you'd like to call her, she'll tell you anything you'd like to know about the house.

Or you can call me.

I look forward to your return.

Always,

Winston

The man just wouldn't give up!

Mallory was going to call the real estate agent, all right—to tell her she wanted nothing to do with the transaction.

Had Reed spoken to Winston yet? Were he and Griff safe?

Coming up beside her, Hank said, "Phone call in the barn. It's your husband."

Stuffing the letter, brochure and contract into the envelope, she rushed into the barn and picked up the cordless phone. "Hi," she said breathlessly.

"Hi, yourself. How's everything on the Double Crown?"

She wanted to say "lonely" even though there were people all around her. But instead she answered, "Quiet. Are you all right? How did it go with Winston?"

"I can't be sure yet. He didn't agree to anything, of course. But there's enough information in that report to cause him serious damage, one way or another. He won't dare try anything now. His position is too precarious. When I get back, Ryan, Griff and I will put our heads together to make sure he gets what he deserves."

She didn't know if Winston Bentley IV backed off from anything. She could tell Reed about the contract, but this was something she needed to take care of herself. "When are you coming home?"

"Tonight. But we'll probably be late."

"Ryan won't let me spend any time at the cabin alone. Will you pick me up when you get back no matter what time it is?"

After a pause he asked, "Are you saying you'd rather spend the night with me than in one of Ryan and Lily's beautiful bedrooms?"

"That's exactly what I'm saying."

He laughed. "All right. I'll see you tonight then."

I miss you, almost slipped out. *I love you,* almost slipped out. But she didn't want to push Reed or pressure him. If she just had more time with him maybe he'd think about taking her home with him.

That thought startled her so much she said, "See you later," then hung up.

Would she really consider going to Australia and forgetting about a life in Texas?

Winston stood in George Pennington Smythe's office, his anger raging just below the surface. It didn't matter what Reed Fortune did or said. He couldn't prove a thing. And it would be easy to further intimidate anyone whom Bentley Inc. had bought out. Maybe the house would be enough to lure Mallory back to San Francisco, but he couldn't take any chances. He had to stay calm and put together a plan.

Fortune hadn't reacted to the mention of Mallory's inheritance—the check George had sent her. Winston sensed the Australian didn't know about it. He certainly didn't know about the house, yet. Mallory should have gotten those papers today. If he could make Fortune believe she was coming back to San Francisco, he'd turn away from her. A man such as Reed Fortune was loyal and honest to a fault. He'd want any woman of his to be the same. Winston would bet his life on it. He'd taken lots of gambles, he'd might as well try a last one here.

All he had to do was drive a wedge between Mallory and her new husband.

Mallory's stepfather knew nothing about the tactics he used to get what he wanted, and that's the way he intended to keep it. Winston needed George on his side. "You should have seen Reed Fortune standing in my office, threatening me. I'll tell you, George, that man could be dangerous. I mean, I keep myself in good shape, but if he wouldn't do it himself, I wouldn't put it past him to have thugs come after me in some dark alley. We've got to get Mallory away from him."

"I just don't know what to do about her. She's so high-strung. You should have heard her after I sent her that check, telling me she'd frame it. I think she meant it, too."

Winston analyzed the situation again. If she had decided to frame the check, she'd still have it. According to his investigator, that cabin wasn't very large, and Fortune might very well know where she'd keep it. Even if he didn't.... "I think we've been going about this the wrong way, George. We've been trying to convince Mallory to do something she doesn't want to do. That doesn't work with her."

"But what else can we do?" George asked.

"We need to turn her so-called husband against her. Then maybe he'll want to get out of this marriage as fast as he got into it."

"What do you have in mind?"

"Nothing complicated. Very simple, actually. I'm going to call him and tell him about your check and the house I'm buying her. If he thinks she's going to return to her life here, he might think she's lied to him about wanting a life in Texas—or in Australia or anywhere else. I don't know if it'll work, but it's certainly worth a try."

"It seems almost too easy," George said with a smile.

"Sometimes the easiest plans are the best ones. It probably wouldn't hurt if you went down there for a visit. What do you think?"

"I'll make the plane reservations right now."

The morning after Reed's return home, Mallory lay in bed with him. He nuzzled her neck, and she sighed contentedly. They'd kissed and made love most of the night. Once when Reed had dozed off, lying on his stomach, she'd awakened him by putting butterfly kisses around the crown birthmark on his back. He'd rewarded her by rolling over, pulling her to him and giving her pleasure such as she'd never known. She loved him so.

"We didn't get much sleep last night," she mused.

"Are you complaining?" he asked, propping himself up on an elbow.

She smiled at him. "Nope."

"You could go back to sleep while I'm up at the barn."

"I have an appointment this morning." She'd promised Matilda that she'd take her out driving. Matilda had an international driver's license, but she needed practice driving on the opposite side of the road than she was used to. Since she didn't want her brothers to know what she was doing until she was proficient, Mallory had agreed to keep their outing a secret.

"An appointment?"

"With Matilda. We have some things to do."

"In San Antonio?"

"I'm not sure yet."

She didn't like being evasive with Reed. Soon Matilda would tell him about it herself. When he didn't ask more questions, Mallory wrapped her arms around Reed's neck and her lips met his. Hunger for each other took the place of thoughts, and they came together again as they had most of the night.

An hour later, after Reed had left with a last prolonged kiss, Mallory dressed, humming to herself as she did. She was in love and the feeling was wonderful! She'd thought about the idea of moving to Australia. She'd do anything to be near Reed—if he wanted her. She could open a shop in Sydney!

Seeing her overnight bag on the floor by the nightstand, she unzipped it and spotted the house brochure Winston had sent her. Yesterday, after she'd torn up the contract along with Winston's letter, she'd tried to call the real estate agent, but the agent was out of the office. By the time Reed had gotten back last night, the agent hadn't returned her call. Time to try again to eradicate this last connection to Winston.

But as she looked at her watch, she realized it was

too early to call now with the time difference. She'd do it after she returned from Matilda's driving lesson. Putting the brochure into her desk, she then collected her purse and left the cabin.

It was late morning when Reed entered the tack room for a saddle. He wondered again what Mallory was up to with Matilda. Soon enough he'd get it out of one of them. He looked forward to tonight when he and Mallory would share that bed again.

The phone in the barn rang, and he went to answer it. "Double Crown," he said automatically.

"Fortune? This is Winston Bentley."

Reed wondered if it was dumb luck Bentley had reached him directly or if he had a spy lurking around. "What do you want?"

"You went to a lot of trouble to collect the information you handed to me. It's a shame you wasted your time."

"If you have something to say, just say it."

"Mallory is going to be coming back to me, no matter who you talk to."

"When hell freezes over."

"I suspect much sooner than that. Has she told you about the house I'm buying her?"

Mallory hadn't mentioned anything about a house. Was Bentley bluffing?

When Reed didn't answer immediately, Bentley added, "And did she tell you about the check her stepfather sent her?"

Reed wanted to shout, *What house? What check?* But he wouldn't give Bentley the satisfaction.

"Ask her, Fortune. If she tells you she tore up the

check, then maybe you *have* won. But since the amount constitutes enough of her inheritance to make her feel like a princess, I think that's highly unlikely. It could be Mallory doesn't want or need your interference anymore.''

Reed hardly noticed the click of the phone as Bentley hung up. The man had to be crazy.

Didn't he?

But then Reed thought about Mallory's background—how she'd been a virtual prisoner at the ranch the past few weeks, how she'd chafed under his protection. The night of the rodeo, she'd been planning to move out, and just because they'd spent a lot of time in bed since didn't mean she'd changed her plans. Now that he'd thought about it, maybe he *had* ridden into her life like a cowboy on a white horse. How many times had she told him she didn't want his protection? She'd only taken advantage of it since it was the expedient thing to do. And now....

True, he could ask her about the check, but he didn't know when she'd be back. Maybe she wasn't with his sister after all. Maybe—

Cutting off his thoughts, he decided to go back to the cabin and take a look around. Then maybe he'd get an answer whether or not Bentley was deluded or just trying to cause trouble.

He pulled into the driveway of the adobe and screeched to a stop, dust trailing in his wake. When he unlocked the door, he deactivated the security system. Looking around, he couldn't help but notice again all of Mallory's touches. She'd added so much brightness to his life.

There was only one place she'd probably keep the

check if she didn't have it with her. Pulling out the supports, he dropped the lid on the secretary. His chest tightened when he saw the real estate brochure and the house pictured on it. It was in San Francisco. Had all Mallory's protestations about being independent and settling in San Antonio been a lie? Is this why she hadn't wanted him to go see Bentley?

His heart pounding, Reed leafed through the other papers stacked in the desk. There was the budget for a shop she could open anywhere. Then he saw it— the incriminating evidence—an envelope with her stepfather's return address. Picking it up, he took it out, read the letter and stared at the check. Then he saw when it was dated. Why hadn't she told him about it? And why had she kept it?

Taking it over to the table, he laid it there. Then he made a pot of coffee and sat down to wait.

When Mallory came in, she was obviously surprised to see him. ''Hi, there. I thought you'd be up at the barn.''

''Did you? Tell me something, Mallory. Were you really with Matilda?''

She frowned. ''Yes, I was with Matilda. What's the matter?''

After he pushed back his chair and stood, he pointed to the envelope with the check on the table and to the real estate brochure. ''When were you going to tell me Bentley is buying you a house in San Francisco? And that you'll have a bit of pocket money to furnish it?''

Her eyes widened. ''What are you accusing me of, Reed?''

He raked his hand through his hair. ''That's just

it, isn't it? I can't accuse you of anything. We only have a fake marriage, so I suppose it doesn't matter if you hide things from me, or you lie to me.''

Her shoulders straightened and her chin came up. ''I haven't lied. Not about anything. There's a reason I kept that check.''

''Other than to cash it?'' he asked cynically.

''You think I'd cash it after all the things I told you the past few weeks? You think I'd cash it when you know how much I want to be independent from my parents?''

''As your stepfather said in his letter, you can be very independent with that amount.''

''Married to Winston? Reed, what's happening to you? Why are you doubting what I told you?''

''It's easy to doubt when the proof's in front of my nose.''

Where before she had looked confused and hurt, now he recognized sparks of anger in her hazel eyes. ''If you can't trust me or accept my word, we don't even have a *fake* marriage.'' Keys still in her hand, she spun around, walked out and slammed the door behind her.

Reed glanced at the check again and then with a loud oath, slammed his fist down on the table.

With tears rolling down her cheeks, Mallory left the Double Crown and turned onto the main highway. Then she drove, not on the back roads where she'd supervised Matilda's driving this morning, but on the main highway. When she saw the sign to Leather Bucket, she turned and headed for the small town. She didn't really care where she was going. The wind blew in her window, ruffling her hair as she tried to sort her thoughts.

But only one thought kept making itself clear—Reed didn't trust her. Apparently he hadn't felt any of the love she'd tried to give him. If he had, he never would have doubted her, never would have believed she'd go back to Winston.

She drove through Leather Bucket, passing a twenty-four-hour diner and the other businesses on the main street. But she kept going. Reaching a main thoroughfare, she headed for San Antonio, parked, and walked along the river. She remembered all too well the night she'd come here with Reed and they'd met with Gwen and Zane. She remembered every minute of these last few weeks with Reed…except for their wedding ceremony and her first night in bed with him. Maybe she'd *never* remember that. Right now she wished she could block out the rest of it, too. She never knew love could hurt so much.

It was after dark when she returned to the Double Crown. She couldn't go back to the adobe. Without thinking twice, she went to Ryan and Lily's. Rosita had left for the day, and Lily answered the door herself. When she saw Mallory's face, she said, "Come inside and tell me what's wrong."

Mallory knew she couldn't do that without crying. Matilda came into the room then, took one look at her and asked, "What has my brother done now?"

Mallory's tears began falling then, and they didn't stop for quite a while. Finally drained, she sat in the guest bedroom where she'd spent the nights when Reed was away and told Lily and Matilda exactly what had happened. She started at the beginning from her first dance with Reed at the Golden Spur, through Winston trying to kidnap her, to this past weekend when she realized just how very much she loved her husband.

"But you didn't tell him, did you?" Matilda asked.

"Of course, I didn't tell him," Mallory erupted. "How could I tell him when he's still in love with Stephanie and he's going back to Australia?"

Lily and Matilda exchanged a look.

"What?" Mallory asked.

"Most times, it takes men longer than women to realize their feelings," Lily offered.

"Oh, he has feelings, all right. He expressed them in bed."

"Exactly," Matilda agreed.

Mallory was none too happy Reed's sister had agreed with her. "Terrific. So I was convenient for him, a way to get his needs met."

"*All* of his needs," Lily said wisely. "Even the ones he wasn't conscious of. I called him, by the way, while you were drinking your third cup of tea. To tell him you were safe."

"What did he say?" Mallory asked, holding her breath.

"He thanked me. That's all."

Mallory felt as if the bottom had dropped out of her world. "I was just a substitute," she concluded morosely.

Lily came over to sit beside her on the bed. "I don't think you could be anybody's substitute, Mallory, and I think Reed knows that, too. If he doesn't now, he will shortly. Give him a little bit of time to think about everything.''

''But if he thinks I was going to cash that check—''

''If he decides to believe that, then he doesn't deserve you,'' Matilda added.

But that was small comfort when Mallory knew her love for Reed was so high she couldn't see over it and so wide she couldn't see around it, and so deep she couldn't imagine ever letting it go.

For the second night in a row, Reed hardly slept. In the early morning he stood at the kitchen window, watching the sun come up, thinking about his life, analyzing it, searching his soul. Though he thought he'd wanted a future with Stephanie Milton, how much had he really wanted it? How much had he cared for her? He'd decided it was time to settle down, and that she would be an appropriate wife. Was he any better than Winston Bentley who'd decided the same thing about Mallory?

Once he'd met Mallory, he hadn't thought about Stephanie. He'd practically forgotten her.

In a flash of insight, Reed realized he'd never truly loved Stephanie, not the way she deserved to be loved. Apparently she hadn't loved him that way, either. When the right person for her came along, she'd known exactly what she had to do.

Maybe so had he.

Mallory had bowled him over from the first moment he'd seen her. As he'd spent the evening with her at the Golden Spur, subconsciously he'd known she was the woman he needed in his life. That's why he'd asked her to marry him. It didn't have anything to do with sex. Sure, he'd wanted her. She was a beautiful woman. But he'd started caring about her, and falling for her, before he'd even had a chance to realize what was happening.

But what about her? She didn't even remember their wedding ceremony! She'd kept distance between them.... But then, so had he—because he was afraid of wanting her too much, of caring too deeply when he had to return to Australia.

Why had she kept her stepfather's check? Why hadn't he listened when she'd tried to explain? Because he was afraid the explanation would take her out of his life?

What if he asked her to go back to Australia with him?

What if he tried to explain he hadn't known true love until he'd found her?

He had to ask her if she'd go back home with him. Because he couldn't imagine leaving Texas without her.

Waiting until a respectable hour was as difficult as spending the night not sleeping. Thank goodness Lily had phoned him or he would have been out looking for Mallory. Now he just had to figure out what to say to her and how to say it.

After several cups of coffee, he finally got in the pickup and drove to Ryan and Lily's. But there was a limousine sitting outside the house, and Reed's pulse pounded as he wondered if Winston Bentley had come to claim Mallory.

The man would have a fight on his hands if he had. When Reed jabbed at the doorbell, Rosita answered. She shook her head and said, "You're just in time."

Not sure what that meant, Reed hurried to the great room. Mallory was standing by the armoire, looking terribly upset. But it wasn't Winston Bentley standing in the room. It was a tall, husky, gray-haired man, whose voice was raised in anger. "You *will* come home with me, Mallory. You've obviously spent the night here. You're not even living with Reed Fortune. I'm going to have this marriage annulled."

It didn't take a master investigator to figure out that this was Mallory's stepfather. Reed wasn't letting the man take Mallory anywhere. In a voice not as loud but just as firm Reed broke in, "There's not a judge anywhere who will annul our marriage. Mallory and I are husband and wife in every sense of the word. And I will never let her go...unless she wants to go."

Mallory's gaze collided with Reed's. It was a few very long moments until she asked, "Are you saying that because you want to protect me or because you really care about me?"

"I've been so stupid, Mallory," he answered, knowing he had to bare his heart or lose her. "I've been kidding myself, pretending all I want is to protect you and to keep you safe, when what I really want is to be married to you. My engagement was—" He shook his head, knowing he had to explain there were no feelings left for Stephanie. "It was a rite of passage. Something I felt I should do. I didn't know what true love was until I found you. I love you, Mallory. I want you to come to Australia with me. I want you to make a life with me. Will you?''

Mallory looked as stunned as George Pennington Smythe looked baffled. But she recovered sooner than her stepfather, and she ran toward Reed, flinging her arms around his neck. ''I'll go anywhere with you. I love you. I've loved you since…since that night in Reno. I don't want Winston's house. He was going to put my name on the title. I tore up the contracts, but I kept the brochure to call the agent to make sure she knew the truth. And I intended to frame George's check, not cash it. I wanted to keep it as a symbol of my independence.''

He should have known Mallory's explanations would have to do with her independence. ''What *about* your independence?'' he asked, not wanting her to give up anything, knowing she'd always want to do some things on her own, just to prove she could.

Her voice became tender. ''I can be independent, but I can be a partner, too. I can let myself need you because I know in some ways you need me. I want to share the rest of my life with you, Reed.''

He hauled her up against him then, and kissed her with the fervor of his desire and the depth of his love. Nothing was ever going to come between them again.

Making sure he wasn't dreaming, wanting to be certain Mallory's answer was real, he pulled away and gazed into her eyes. There were tears there, tears of joy, and he knew he held everything he had ever wanted in this life in his arms.

Barely aware of what was going on around him, he saw Matilda and Lily come in from the courtyard.

Lily patted George's arm and suggested, "Why don't you come have breakfast with us and get to know your son-in-law? If you don't want to lose Mallory, you'd better start listening to her and her wishes."

The pause only underscored Lily's words.

Finally George Pennington Smythe said, "He does seem like the type of man who will protect Mallory through hell or high water. I don't believe that there's any way her mother and I can convince her otherwise."

As Brody and Griff came into the great room from the hall, Reed bent his head to Mallory for another kiss, not caring if the whole world watched.

Epilogue

In the midst of lists, pictures of wedding cakes and travel brochures, Mallory sat cross-legged on the bed in the cabin, waiting for Reed. She had something special to tell him. She'd thought of going up to the barn, but she wanted to tell him here, where they could be alone. So she'd busied herself all day with wedding preparations.

Lily and Ryan insisted on giving them a *real* wedding. Reed's parents were going to fly over for the occasion. Mallory was looking forward to meeting Fiona and Teddy Fortune in person, though they'd spoken on the phone at more length since she and Reed were now truly together. After their wedding reception, she and Reed were to honeymoon in Australia, and then return to the Double Crown for a while so she could spend more time with Dawson before she started her new life in Australia with her husband.

Checking the clock, she thought she really should get supper started, but before she could move, Reed came through the door with a small package in his hand. He grinned when he saw her, and her heart leaped just looking at him. If the past three weeks were any indication, the rest of their lives was going to be one uninterrupted honeymoon.

"Hi," she said softly.

"Hi, yourself," he returned with that look in his eyes that told her supper was going to be postponed. But as he came toward the bed, he held out a six-inch-long box wrapped with silver paper, adorned with a white bow.

"What is this?" she asked.

"It's a wedding present. I had it delivered to Ryan and Lily's so I could wrap it for you."

He always took such tender care of her and cherished her.

"Open it," he ordered.

She took off the bow and placed it on the picture of the wedding cake she liked. Then she tore off the paper and found a blue velvet box. Opening it, she gasped when she saw the necklace and earrings. Opals and diamonds against black velvet reminded her of all the stars in the sky, and the nights she and Reed had spent sleeping under them. "Oh, Reed. They're beautiful."

"I knew exactly what I wanted. I called the jeweler in Sydney and he sent them."

"Thank you so much. I want to keep them and wear them on our wedding day for the first time."

"Whatever you want." He gave her a long kiss, then raised his head. His voice was husky when he said, "I got a call from George today. He's pleased you asked him to walk you down the aisle."

Before her stepfather had returned to San Francisco, he'd read the information that Reed had gathered on Winston Bentley and finally understood the type of man Winston was. Since then, George had cut off all of his business dealings with him and was taking steps to see that the man was prosecuted for his tactics. But Mallory didn't want to think about her stepfather now. Something else much more important was on her mind.

"I have a present for you, too," she said.

"Oh?" Reed raised one brow.

"You were gone this morning before I woke up, so I couldn't tell you. After we made love last night, I had a very special dream. I was standing in a room painted all white, with silver bells hanging from the ceiling. There were chairs with pink velvet seats and a justice of the peace with wire-rimmed glasses perched on the tip of his nose. His wife was dressed in lavender, and she was our witness."

Reed's expression had changed, and there was emotion in his eyes.

Mallory went on. "I remember our wedding ceremony, Reed. I remember you telling me that you'd honor and love me and cherish me forever. And I remember telling you the same. My heart knew all along that I belong with you, and now that we're going to profess our love in front of the whole world, my memory's caught up with my heart."

Taking the opal necklace and earrings from her hands, he carefully laid the box on the nightstand. Then he pushed lists, brochures and pictures to the floor as he lay beside her and enfolded her in his arms. "I love you," he said, gazing into her eyes, making sure she knew exactly what he felt and how much her love meant to him.

''I love you, too,'' she returned, eager to marry him again, eager to start on the road to their future.

*   *   *   *   *

The romance you'd want

Escape into

Silhouette

DESIRE®

Intense, sensual love stories.

Desire™ are short, fast and sexy romances featuring alpha males and beautiful women. They can be intense and they can be fun, but they always feature a happy ending.

The romance you'd want

Escape into

Silhouette

SPECIAL EDITION®

Vivid, satisfying romances, full of family, life and love

Special Editions are romances between attractive men and women. Family is central to the plot. The novels are warm upbeat dramas grounded in reality with a guaranteed happy ending.

The romance you'd want

Escape into

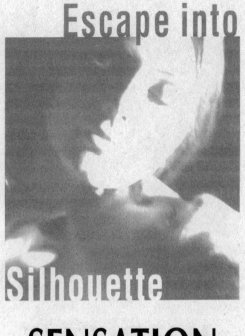

Silhouette

SENSATION ®

Passionate, dramatic, thrilling romances

Sensation™ are sexy, exciting, dramatic and thrilling romances, featuring dangerous men and women strong enough to handle them.

The romance you'd want

Escape into

Silhouette

INTRIGUE™

Danger, deception and suspense.

Romantic suspense with a well-developed mystery.
The couple always get their happy ending, and the
mystery is resolved, thanks to the central couple.

▼™ SILHOUETTE
SENSATION®

presents a new heart-pounding
twelve-book series:

A Year of Loving Dangerously

**When a top secret agency is threatened, twelve of the best
agents in the world put their lives—and their hearts—on
the line. But will justice…and true love…prevail?**